PROTECTING EVERLEIGH

A STEAMY, SMALL-TOWN ROMANTIC
SUSPENSE

GHOST LEGACY
BOOK 4

PJ FIALA

DEDICATION

I've had so many wonderful people come into my life and I want you all to know how much I appreciate it. From each and every reader who takes the time out of their days to read my stories and leave reviews, thank you.
My beautiful, smart and fun Road Queens, who play games with me, post fun memes, keep the conversation rolling and help me create these captivating characters, places, businesses and more. Thank you ladies for your ideas, support and love. The following characters and places were created by:
Nicky Ortiz - **GHOST Headquarters** - The HOG (Home, Office and Garage)
House name ideas
Amy Ball - The Stitchery
Deb Jones Diem - Hemmed In
Kerry Harteker - Mending Box
Karen Cranford LeBeau - Button Down
Julia Murphy - Zipped Tight
Gail Whitley - Needle Point
Dana Zamora - Sown Home

People:

Alana Ackerman - Ryhs

Liz Bradley - Officer Maria Bradley

Tjuana TJ Brown - Shianne Brown

Lyne Carroll & Belinda Jackson Hercule -Elena Dorsey

Cathy Christmas – Helissa, GHOST Cook

Tami Czenkus - Stella Delany

Terri DeMario - Flynn DeMario

Marie Evans - Case Evans

Anna Marie Flamini - Amelia (childhood friend of Elena)

Peggy Fowler and Sharon R. Cowan - Kenna Lawrence

Kerry Harteker - Elena's mom's health issues

Stacy Hartley - Marina Hayes

Belinda Jackson Hercule - Sharon Jackson

Ginna Honeycutt - Officer Carter Gordon

Beckie Johnson Lowe - Colt Lowe

Nathalie Juergensen - Daniel Juergensen

Killaine Kennedy - Niya Lawrence

Kristi Hombs Kopydlowski - Lara Bennit and Troy Brown

Kim Kurtz - Howie Lawrence, Geoffrey Kurtz

Karen Cranford LeBeau - Klaire Brown, Aidyn Dunbar,
Sheriff Rex Cranford and Millie LeBeau

Kristi Malloy - Zachary Malloy

Elinda Moody - Keaton Bennit

Monique Mousseau - Spencer Lawson

Julia Murphy - Atty. Peter Murphy, Alan

Terra Oenning - Mayor Rayleigh Winters, Perry DeWitt

Nicky Ortiz - Explosives Expert from Brookswood - Dylan

Cindy Pearson - Ami Pearson

Pamela Reveal - Matthew Vickers

Cay Krueger Scheumack - Zahn Krueger

Wendy Simek - Carson Simek

Jayne Smith - Atty. Francesca Smith
Yolanda Tobiasen - Laylah Bennit
Elizabeth Ward Sadowsky - Chesson Ward
Jo West - Baxter Fenshaw
Dana Zamora - Sean and Jonathon Lawrence, Zander Zamora
Jessica Zoe - Grace Dorsey
Debbie Zsidai - Dr. Emily Zsidai

Places:
Amy Barber - Fort Abraham
Kim Kurtz - Glen Hollow
Kathy Franklin - Hickory Hills
Monique Mousseau Westwood - Brookswood

Glen Hollow businesses -
Abigail Capps - Paxton's General Store
Abigail Capps - Squeaky Clean Laundromat
Nancy Hoch - Homemade in the Hollow, Stackable Reads Bookstore
Nathalie Juergensen - Hairy Beards and The Broken Barrel
Beckie Johnson Lowe - Chestnut Grove
Nicky Ortiz - Divine Designs, Lady Liberty Law Office, The Paper Trail, Porter's Steakhouse, Picket Fence Realty, Homeland Guest House
Anne Walker - Lara's Delights
Jo West - Bloomin' Lovely
PJF - Smith Squared Attorneys at Law

Horse Names
Holli Kohls - Harper

Arlene Miklovic - Lady
Michelle Terry - Diamond
Pam James - Miss Penny Mae
Stacy Harley - Jazzy
Monique Mousseau Westwood - Sugar
Nancy Kehl - Queenie
Marlene Davis - Sallie

Black Road Resistance (BRR)
Jamie Rogers - BRR Black Road Resistance
Ronda Barnes-Howard - Everett Howard
Tami Czenkus - Carson
Marlene Davis - Hanalore Howard
Sally Harris - Brock Harris
Ginna Honeycutt - Cole Honeycutt
Lynne Kerr - Gerard Weston
Karen Cranford LeBeau - Brenner Matthews, Ramsey Stewart
Beckie Johnson Lowe - Brayden Lowe
Lisa Mansfield - Reece Mansfield
Mary Lou Melzer - Kent Bennit
Arlene Miklovic - Liliana Weston
Margaret Park Mathias - Waylon and Duffy Park
Julie Ann Price - Liam Price
Jayne Smith - Theresa and Craig Howard
Jo West - Jasiah Weston
Debbie Zsidai - Medicine Woman - Elenor

Last but not least, my family for the love and sacrifices they have made and continue to make to help me achieve this dream, especially my husband and best friend, Gene. Words can never express how much you mean to me.

To our veterans and current serving members of our armed forces, police and fire departments, thank you ladies and gentlemen for your hard work and sacrifices; it's with gratitude and thankfulness that I mention you in this forward.

DESCRIPTION

When the job can only be handled by a team that doesn't exist, you call GHOST.

He was raised to be a GHOST operative.

She's an Army-trained, skilled negotiator.

Together they play a game of push and pull—until she finds herself in need of his protection.

Henry Delany inherited his father's muscular frame and his mother's penchant for the law. Working for GHOST gives him the opportunity to use both while doing what he loves—protecting the lives of others. Determined to bring tranquility and harmony to Glen Hollow, the small town he now calls home, he has agreed to work with a closed-off government liaison in an effort to broker a peace deal. But *Protecting Everleigh* just might be Henry's most challenging mission to date.

Everleigh Hayes was raised to be a negotiator, and Glen Hollow, Kentucky is a small town in need of a truce. She is just the woman to make that happen. Like her previous assignments, she approaches this one with her finely-tuned grace and finesse. But when Everleigh comes face-to-face with the undercurrent of darkness permeating this little town, she finds herself ensnared by more danger than she's ever faced. Needing Henry and falling in love with him is a development she's never negotiated before.

———

Protecting Everleigh is the fourth novel in the GHOST Legacy Romantic Suspense Series, although all books in the GHOST Legacy world can be read as a stand-alone. A steamy romantic story with a guaranteed happily ever after, it does have some strong language and exciting sexy times. Enjoy Henry and Everleigh!

GLOSSARY - GHOST LEGACY

The kids from GHOST are all grown up and living lives of their own. Meet these men and women of GHOST Legacy:

Tate Vickers - Tate is the son of Gaige and Sophie Vickers. Their story is told in Defending Sophie. Tate is a recon specialist and runs the GHOST satellite office.

Aidyn Dunbar - Is the son of Bridget and Axel Dunbar. You can find their story is Defending Bridget. Aidyn's specialty is sharpshooter and recon.

Spencer Lawson - Spencer is the son of Wyatt and Yvette Lawson. You can read their story in Defending Yvette. Spencer specialize's in security, recon and recovery.

Henry Delany - Henry is the son of Hawk and Roxanne Delany. Their story is told is Defending Roxanne. His specialties are recon, recovery, and anything that requires size.

Adelaide Masters - Adelaide's parents are Josh and Isabella Masters. Their story is told in Defending Isabella. Adelaide served in the Army and is the team's medic.

Maya Sager - Maya served in the US Marine Corps.

Her parents are Dodge and Jax Sager. Their story is told in Finding His Jewel. Maya's specialty is recon and rescue.

Myles Sager - Myles served in the US Marine Corps. Myles and Maya are the twins of Dodge and Jax Sager. Myles is an explosives expert.

Henry Delany looked up the mountain road that led to Hickory Hills where the Black Road Resistance resided. They'd been nothing but trouble since he and his teammates had come to town more than a year ago. They'd set off explosions, cut wires, raided and damaged businesses, shot at them, fought with them and generally been pains in the ass.

"What are you looking at?" Myles Sager, one of his teammates, asked.

"Just wondering when all this will be over with the BRR."

Myles chuckled. "Aren't you protecting the negotiator?"

He glanced at Myles, and grinned. "When she gets here. But these things can take a while."

Myles nodded. "Okay. Well, let's hope she can work something out with them sooner rather than later."

"Yeah." As he turned toward the trailer that served as the office on the construction site, his phone rang. Pulling it from his back pocket, he glanced at the readout, surprised to see the number of a realtor he'd spoken to yesterday.

"Delany."

"Hi, Henry, this is Zander Zamora. From Picket Fence Realty. Your verbal offer has been accepted."

Henry stopped in his tracks, his eyes following Myles as he continued toward the construction trailer.

Struggling to get his mind around the words he'd just heard, he swallowed the enormous lump that clogged his throat and took in two deep breaths. He felt light-headed and his mouth wouldn't work. Words. He needed to say words. But his brain wouldn't engage, and he felt as though he were trying to conjure foreign words he didn't understand.

"Are you there, Henry? Isn't that exciting?"

Now this was an answer he had words for. He cleared his throat, taking an extra second to recover his thoughts. "Ah, yes, I'm here."

"So, exciting, right? I can bring the paperwork to you or make an appointment for you to come to the office and sign them. Which works best for you?"

"Uh..." His eyes shifted to the construction trailer, which now felt as though it had moved a mile down the road. "I, um, can I call you back?"

"Sure thing. You've got my number. But we'll need to get this offer written up in the next few hours so Mr. DeWitt doesn't change his mind."

"Yeah, okay, will do." Of course, he found more words just as the line went dead with an old-school click of Zamora's desk phone. He pulled his phone away from his ear, gulping large lungfuls of air as he searched for a place to sit down. What in the ever-loving hell had just happened? Not only had he not placed a verbal offer, but it was accepted?

He dragged his feet to the edge of the nearest building on the grounds, the newly constructed barracks which would hold the incoming troops in a few short months. A construction tote pushed against the building called to him and he sank onto it. Holding his phone in front of him, he scrolled through the texts between himself and Zander, to see how the hell he'd gotten the idea he'd made a verbal offer. He'd always assumed one day he'd purchase a farm like his parents had. A hobby farm, a place to unwind, with work that would physically tire him out but also, let his mind rest. It's how he grew up. His parents bought a hobby farm before he was born. Every spare minute, they went to the farm. Sometimes, he and his mom would stay there while his dad was out on missions.

And, sure he'd looked at the old DeWitt farm two days ago. It needed a shit-ton of work. The old man, Perry, had let it go for the past fifteen years. It would be a project, a good project. While he was still an operative, he'd work on the physical buildings and fences, so when he was finally ready to retire he'd have a few chickens, a cow or two, and maybe a dog. He really wanted a dog. A Belgian Malinois. A badass, gorgeous dog that would guard the property and the animals, be company for him in the evenings. It was a great dream, but it wasn't today's dream.

Bringing his head back to the current situation, he scrolled through the texts sent back and forth after he'd looked at the farm. Definitely nothing there that intimated a verbal offer.

He needed to clear his head and think about this. Contacting the agent while he was confused would get him nowhere. His heart was still racing like a horse down the track, and he needed to think about work, or anything other than the farm, for a while. Standing, he decided to patrol the perimeter again.

He rounded the corner of the barracks and followed the path he'd worn through the brush from all of his perimeter checks. Focusing on the ground helped him calm down. Work. That was it.

Something glinted in the sunlight, and he froze. Taking a moment, he inched closer to the object and froze once again. Pulling his phone from his pocket, he tapped Myles' picture.

"I thought you were right behind me."

"I was but decided to walk the perimeter. I need you out here. Explosive device. I'm on the west side of the base, behind the containers. Bring gear."

"Roger." The line went dead, and Henry scanned the area for wires or triggers. Anything that might set this thing off.

Sucking in a deep breath, he exhaled slowly. He wanted something to redirect his thoughts, and it looked like he'd found it. Fortunately, before it found him.

He turned slowly when he heard footsteps approaching from behind him. When Myles stepped closer to him, he pointed to the shiny object on the ground.

"Okay, back away and let me do my thing, bud." Myles quipped.

"Do you need me to do anything for you?" Henry asked.

"Just keep everyone away from here and keep your phone close."

Henry followed Myles' orders. After all, Myles was their explosives expert. And he was good at it. Very good.

Henry stepped to the other side of the shipping container, phone in hand, and surveyed the area to ensure no one trampled through.

"Henry?" Myles called.

"Yeah."

"Alert everyone to an impending explosion then get me some of the rubber bolsters from the storage shed."

"Roger."

He jogged toward the construction office and flung open the door to find their construction manager at his desk. Baxter Fenshaw's head whipped around, his eyes wide.

"Impending explosion, Baxter. Let the crew know. Behind the storage container on the west side of the site."

"Will do."

Henry ran to the construction shed and muscled three heavy rubber bolsters—large rubber blankets used to muffle the blast and contain the debris—onto one of the UTVs on site. He hurried toward Myles and the explosive device, jumping off the UTV as he neared the side of the storage container.

"Myles?"

"Yeah."

"I've got the bolsters."

"Okay. Bring them around one at a time."

He hefted the first bolster over his shoulder and crept behind the container.

Myles stood and took the bolster from him. "Grab the next one please."

Henry took off to the UTV, his heart pumping wildly. Sweat beading on his temple as he muscled the final two bolsters back to Myles.

"Last one, Myles."

Myles turned toward him, sweat trickling down his face. The neckline of his t-shirt was darkened with moisture. "Okay, bud. Turn the UTV around and get ready to take off as soon as I jump in."

Henry turned the UTV around, his foot poised over the gas pedal. The heat permeated his skin and clothing. How was it possible to be this hot? Myles' footsteps pounded a steadily increasing beat as he ran toward him and he lowered his foot to rest right on the gas pedal. The instant Myles jumped into the UTV, he pushed his foot to the floor and they sped toward the construction office. Gravel shot back behind the UTV, he could hear the pinging as the stones hit the trailer. Merely four yards away from the construction trailer, the explosion filled the air, and the concussion pounded through his chest.

2

H omeland Guest House was not exactly what Everleigh was expecting when she pulled into the parking lot of what the DoD claimed was the only hotel in Glen Hollow. It looked to be an old home, well-restored, and apparently added on to. A combination bed-and-breakfast and hotel. Interesting. The parking lot was about half full, which she appreciated. She hated being the only guest in a place, but she also didn't want to share it with the entire town. The flowers in the planters around the property were well-kept, vibrant, and gave her hope the inside would be just as nice.

Pulling her suitcase behind her, she hefted her laptop higher on her shoulder, and not for the first time today regretted wearing her business suit on the drive, but she was taught to always be prepared to present herself in the best possible light. Plus, she didn't travel with unnecessary clothing. The end of June in Wisconsin, where her last assignment had been, was still cooler in the mornings. She should have taken that extra minute to check the weather details before leaving Wisconsin.

Stepping through the automatic glass doors, the air conditioning caused goosebumps to rise on her arms and she shivered as the cool air circled around her, settling on her dampened skin. The aroma of fresh flowers and cookies reached her, and her stomach growled. All she'd had for breakfast was a meal replacement shake. And not a good one. The wet cardboard taste still lingered in her mouth. She swallowed hoping to wash the memory away.

The young woman behind the desk smiled. "Hello. Welcome to Homeland Guest House. How can I help you?"

Everleigh returned her smile. "Thank you. Everleigh Hayes. I have a reservation."

The young woman, Sarah according to her name tag, nodded and began typing into her computer. "Yes. I have you on the second floor. And it looks like your reservation is open-ended. No check-out date at this time."

"Yes ma'am, that's correct."

The printer hummed and Sarah reached below her and brought up two sheets of paper. "I just need you to sign here." She drew an x next to a line. "And enter your license plate number here." She x'd a line opposite her signature. "And I need to see some ID please."

Everleigh pulled her driver's license from her wallet and signed the paper before her. Adding her license plate number, she turned the paperwork back to Sarah and smiled.

"You're in room 223 and the elevators are just to the left of us here. We have breakfast in that room back there," Sarah pointed to a room behind her, "from six till nine every morning."

The perky clerk held up her forefinger, then turned and stepped into a room behind the desk. She reappeared within a minute with a fresh hot chocolate chip cookie on a small paper plate.

"Welcome." She smiled.

"Thank you." The aroma of the hot cookie wafted up to her nose and her stomach grumbled a bit. Her shoulders relaxed slightly, the stress from the drive and the unknown beginning to ease out of her body. Everleigh grabbed the key on the desk, and her cookie, then pulled her suitcase toward the elevator.

When she opened the door to her room, she let out a sigh of relief. The room was clean, bright, and pretty. She'd be fine here. She shivered again, remembering some of the less than savory small-town hotels she'd stayed in over the ten*ish* years she'd worked as a negotiator. Always moving from town to town, she'd never had the chance to grow roots anywhere. When she started to feel lonely, she called her sister, putting on a happy face while she talked, and cried in the bathtub for a while afterwards. It was a cycle she was becoming all too familiar with.

Her phone rang just as she'd dropped onto the bed. The readout said, Casper – her boss's code name. She sighed before answering, "Everleigh Hayes."

"It's Casper. Have you made it to Glen Hollow?"

"Yes. I just walked into my room."

"Good. Your security detail is Henry Delany. He's part of the GHOST team located in Glen Hollow and has solid knowledge of the BRR and the negotiations that have gone on since they've arrived.

"You have a meeting with Sheriff Rex Cranford at nine tomorrow morning. Things are a bit lax there as far as the law goes. Special favors are offered to town board members and others, for various infractions. It's not a tight ship. But all parties involved want this negotiation to happen. They want it finalized and they want to move forward."

"I'll do my best, sir. I have the information packet that was sent to me and will spend the remainder of the evening becoming acquainted with the situation."

"Perfect. Henry will be there to pick you up at eight thirty tomorrow morning."

"Thank you, sir." She knew she could drive herself wherever she needed to go—the town was small, she could hardly get lost—but she wasn't about to argue with him, she was raised to respect authority. And he was her direct link to future work.

"If you need anything, give me a call."

"Thank you, sir."

"Good night, Ms. Hayes."

The line went dead before she could respond. She shook her head and laid her phone on the bed next to her. First things, first. She needed to find some food. Then, she'd get to work.

Opening and closing the drawers in the desk and dresser in her room, she found a list of local restaurants, grocery stores, gas stations, and churches. The first restaurant listed was Homemade in the Hollow. Too tired to be picky, she dialed them up and ordered food to be delivered.

After unpacking her clothes and toiletries, she pulled the packet from her laptop case, opened her computer and set herself up to work.

Spinning in her desk chair, she laid the individual packets of the players involved on her bed, separating them out by faction. In this case, the factions were the BRR and the townspeople.

She was studying Craig Howard's—the president of

the BRR—dossier and photos when a knock on her door startled her.

Taking a deep breath, she looked through the peephole, opened her door, and saw the delivery person standing outside. Handing the girl a tip from the money she'd stuffed in her pocket, she took the warm bag of food and inhaled deeply; the aroma filled her room as she carried it inside.

The little table in the corner was still empty of files, so she carried her food to the corner and began unpacking her dinner. Her stomach growled and she took a long drink from the ice-cold sweet tea she'd ordered. *Mmm, so good*.

She sat in the chair and quickly unwrapped the bacon burger she'd ordered. She knew she'd regret it tomorrow but would push herself to work out a bit harder to make up for it. And after taking one bite, she knew it was completely worth it.

3

Henry strode into the lobby of the Homeland Guest House. He wasn't new at this, protection, meeting new people, learning to adjust to their mannerisms. But this first day could easily set the tone for the remainder of this assignment.

A grin spread across his face as he took in the older furniture mixed with modern elements. The sofas were older, vintage even, but the counter at the front desk was sleek and modern. The television on the wall above the fireplace was obviously a modern touch, but the fireplace itself was old stone and brick. It brought back memories of home. His mom was a fanatic about antiques and collectables and their farmhouse was a showpiece of both.

"Hi, how can I help you?"

He turned toward the voice behind the desk. A young woman in her early twenties smiled at him.

"Good morning. I'm here to pick up Everleigh Hayes."

"Would you like me to call her room?"

"Thank you. I appreciate it."

The young woman nodded and tapped on the keys of

her computer. He continued to look around the lobby of the hotel. This was one of the places he hadn't been in town. It was interesting in its mix of old and new.

The clatter of forks and knives tapping against ceramic plates filled the air, drawing his attention to the room behind the fireplace where hotel guests were enjoying breakfast. The aroma of bacon and fried potatoes wrapped around him. If he hadn't just eaten, he'd be hard-pressed not to go in and help himself.

"Henry Delany?"

He whirled around to see a beautiful woman. Long blonde hair flowed over her shoulders in soft waves. Soft green eyes reminded him of summer grass. Her posture was straight and tall, her shoulders pulled back, hinting at some military training for sure. The burgundy business suit she wore belied the softness her eyes emanated. She was a contrast in a good way.

She was thin and tall, his guess around five-foot-nine inches.

"Yes. Good morning." He moved toward her and stretched out his hand. She placed her palm into his and squeezed his hand tightly in a firm handshake that spoke volumes. No wimpy, flimsy handshake, here. She was poised, and polished, and exuded confidence. "Ms. Hayes, I presume."

Her full lips turned up and her face radiated a beauty only accentuated by her presence. Quite simply, she was breathtaking.

"Yes. Everleigh Hayes. Thank you for picking me up. I didn't want to argue with Casper, but honestly, I'm quite capable of driving myself around to meetings."

His right shoulder lifted and fell. "I'm just following orders, ma'am."

"Everleigh."

He bobbed his head. "Everleigh."

Her throat constricted as she swallowed and he stepped aside, gesturing toward the front of the building, a silent but respectful, "after you."

She gave him a curt nod and glided past him and to the door. Well, off to a great start. At least he thought so. She seemed professional, and elegant. Plus, she was stunning. Off to a good start indeed.

He caught up to her easily, his stride nearly doubled hers, and opened the door of his truck before she got there. His eyes darted to her legs encased in slacks, which would make her stepping into his truck less awkward. He'd watched many women over his years try climbing up into a truck with a tight skirt on and those ungodly heels. How women managed to walk in them was beyond him, but they sure made their legs sexy as hell. He'd always appreciated the shape of a woman's legs stretched tall in high heels.

Everleigh's lips turned down as she stepped into his truck with grace and ease. Was she judging him or his truck? It wasn't a flashy vehicle, practical, a few extra upgrades. It was the largest purchase he'd made to date— unless he counted the farm he may possibly own after yesterday's call from the realtor—and he was pretty damn proud of it. He shook his head and closed the door without a word.

As he settled himself behind the steering wheel he asked, "Where to?"

She consulted the folder she carried, then closed it and replied, "Sheriff Cranford's office."

He started his truck and turned them toward the sheriff's department.

Everleigh broke the short silence as the buildings from the town flowed by. "You know, today is filled with meetings as I gather information from the townspeople here in Glen Hollow. Honestly, I'm capable of driving myself."

He glanced quickly at her, then back to the road. "I don't doubt it. But, I have my orders to protect you, and that's what I'll do."

"Protect me from what? Or who?"

"I'm certain Casper told you how volatile Craig is."

"I won't be anywhere near him today. According to the intelligence I received, he won't even come off the mountain, so I don't think there's any danger in him harming me today."

"Just because he doesn't come off the mountain doesn't mean he won't send men down to do his dirty work. I suspect you represent a permanent loss of power to him, and I'm sure he's not exactly thrilled about that. We simply don't know how he'll react to all of this."

He glanced at her as he drove. Huffing out an exasperated breath, she turned her head and watched the scenery fly by the window in silence. It was going to be a long day.

He decided to make small talk. "I'm a Marine. You know, once a Marine – always a Marine. I detect military training in you. Let me guess – Army?"

Her face turned to his, the soft smile on her lips intriguing. "Yes. Army. How do you detect military and Army?"

He grinned and shrugged his shoulders. "Perfect posture. Strong handshake. Associated with Casper. We share a boss you know. But, your hair is down and soft. Most of the women I knew in the Marines pulled their hair back tightly or cut it off. Basically, it was a guess."

She chuckled and the sound was appealing.

"My parents are also career Army. It was inevitable for me I guess."

Henry turned into the sheriff's department parking lot and found a spot near the front door. He hustled around the truck and opened the door for Everleigh. Always the gentleman, he even held his hand out to her, shocked when she gently placed her hand in his. As they strode toward the front door, he prepped her with a bit of information he wasn't sure would have been relayed by her bosses. But it was definitely essential for her to understand, and he felt a deep need to make sure she was fully in the know.

"The sheriff is a tad lax on the law. His good-old-boy network is strong. He's granted a lot of favors to people in town, and they use them freely. Word to the wise, don't say anything to anyone outside of my team. You simply don't know whose back pockets the sheriff is in."

She stopped in her tracks and turned her head up so her eyes stared directly into his. "Noted." It was clipped and short and his brows shot into his hairline. Then, she added, "I do know how to do my job and I am discreet. What makes you think I'd say anything to anyone?"

Well, shit. He hadn't meant to infer she wasn't discreet. He simply knew the dossier kept by the DoD didn't include little nuances such as lax law enforcement.

"This is a small town that has been rattled to its core. People have a way of getting things out of others. I simply wanted to warn you."

Her tongue slid across her bottom lip, and his eyes tracked it the entire way. It was sexy. She was sexy.

"Thank you for the warning. But I'm a professional. I've done this for close to ten years with an exemplary track record. I didn't earn that by gossiping and sharing secrets."

His face flushed hot, he could feel his ears burning. Her eyes continued to bore into his for a few seconds. It felt like an eternity. His throat grew dry and he wanted to swallow to moisten it, but he didn't want to look scared or weak. And she seemed to be waiting for him to acknowledge her words so he said the only thing he could think of without blistering her ears but good. "Noted."

4

She stretched her legs as far as she could in her heels, silently conveying her irritation that he didn't think she knew how to do her job while also projecting the confidence that had earned her the right to dress him down for doubting her. Her shoulders were tight and she kept her posture straight and tall as she marched to the front desk. The female officer manning the desk looked up at her and smiled before her eyes shot behind her to Henry, her cheeks growing pink.

"Everleigh Hayes here to see Sheriff Cranford."

"Yes, ma'am. You can follow me right into the conference room."

The officer stepped through the half-door at the end of the desk and ushered her toward a room at the end of the hall. She could hear Henry's footsteps behind her and the words to tell him to stay outside screamed through her mind. But he was doing his job, even if she didn't think she needed him hanging around. And he was easy on the eyes, so that was a boon.

The officer opened the door to the conference room

and ushered her inside. Tablets, pens, and water glasses were set up at eight places around the table. All the chairs were pushed in and there was no clutter on the sideboards on the opposite wall. Everything in its place. It was a pleasant surprise.

Henry entered behind her, and she couldn't help but notice how he filled the space. He was a big man. Tall, broad-shouldered, and handsome. She guessed his height at six foot six or so. His t-shirt stretched across his biceps without him even trying to flex the muscle. She was grateful for the air conditioning, because he certainly did raise the temperature of the room.

She sucked in a breath and walked around to the opposite end of the table. Pulling out the chair in front of her, she opened her notebook and pulled her laptop from its case, setting it on the table before her. In her peripheral vision, she saw Henry walk to the end of the room and sit in a chair against the wall. He pulled his phone from his pocket and texted someone.

She turned to look at him, a pang of guilt slicing through her as she thought of how she'd treated him. "I'm sorry. I've had to work twice as hard as men in the same position as me, my entire career. I'm capable and I do a good job, but I usually have to fight everyone in the beginning to convince them I do know what I'm doing. I took it out on you. I know you're just doing your job. I'm sorry I came off so harsh."

His blue eyes locked on hers. The striking contrast between his dark hair and light blue eyes only added to his handsomeness. But beyond that pretty face, she saw understanding. Compassion. It wasn't anger.

His lips curved up into a breath-taking smile. "I appreciate that you've had to fight for your place. My mother was in the same position in her career and my female coworkers have had that same fight in their lives."

She smiled, expecting that to be the end of the conversation.

"But not from me," he continued, catching her off guard. "I work with some of the smartest, most capable, badass women you'll ever meet. And I would never disrespect them, or any woman, by assuming they couldn't do their job because of their gender."

Heat crawled up her body. Embarrassment settled under her arms, making her sweat uncomfortably, and the heat kept rising. Her ears and cheeks burned. She fought the urge to squirm in her seat at her discomfort.

Luckily, she was saved by the sheriff.

"Good morning, everyone." The sheriff nodded in her direction, but turned and walked to Henry and shook his hand first. Her heat turned to anger once again, and she felt a bit vindicated when Henry saw this firsthand.

"Henry, it's good to see you."

"Nice seeing you too, Sheriff."

The sheriff turned and sauntered to the head of the table at her left. Before sitting down, he held out his hand to her and she stood and shook it, firmly squeezing his hand and making direct eye contact with him before she let go.

Satisfaction flared through her body when she saw the pink tint on his cheeks.

She sat once again, and the sheriff blustered with something on his tie then sat uncomfortably. She glanced at Henry, who wore the most gorgeous smile she'd ever seen. His eyes sought hers and she couldn't stop the grin from forming on her lips. He saw it. But he didn't say anything to the sheriff about it. He let her handle it in her way. Points to the blue-eyed knight for not treating her like a damsel in distress.

"Can I get either of you something? Water? Coffee? Juice?"

She smiled. "Water would be wonderful. Thank you."

Sheriff Cranford reached forward to the phone in the middle of the conference table and pushed a button.

"Yes, Sheriff." A faceless voice responded.

"Bring us in some waters, Carrie."

Sheriff Cranford held his hand out toward Henry, who nodded in return.

She booted up her laptop and folded her hands in front of her waiting for the meeting to begin.

The door opened and Carrie entered with a bucket filled with bottled water on ice. She set it on the sideboard behind her, pulled three waters from the bucket, and set two on the table near Everleigh's left arm. She carried the other to Henry in the back of the room, greeting him a bit flirtatiously, "It's nice to see you again, Henry."

"It's nice to see you too, Carrie."

Carrie giggled and Everleigh had to force herself not to roll her eyes.

As Carrie left the room, she gave Henry a last glance, then closed the door. The sheriff busted out laughing and his eyes landed on Henry.

"You have a way with the ladies, Henry."

For his part, Henry's shoulders rose and dropped in a shallow shrug, but the grin on his face irritated her.

5

Henry listened as Everleigh and the sheriff discussed what, from his point of view, he wanted to see happen with the negotiations. Everleigh listened intently, asked pointed questions and wrote things down.

His phone alerted him to a text. Zander Zamora's name appeared and his stomach flopped. He hadn't slept last night thinking about this situation. He stood and glanced at Everleigh first, then the sheriff.

"I have to make a couple of calls. I'll be back soon."

Quickly exiting the building, he jumped in his truck and dialed his mom's phone.

"Hi, honey, how are you?"

"I'm good. How are you and dad doing?"

"We're good. What's going on?"

He settled into his truck seat and put his phone on speaker. "So, a couple of days ago, I looked at a farm here in Glen Hollow. It's run-down. The old man who owns it hasn't been able to keep it up over the past few years. He hasn't had animals for fifteen years or so. His memory has faded."

"Oh, Henry, how wonderful."

"Well, yes and no. I spoke with the realtor, Zander Zamora, and he's pulling a fast one here. He called me yesterday and told me my verbal offer had been accepted. But, I didn't make a verbal offer."

"Oh. Interesting."

"Right. Now he wants me to come in and sign papers."

He heard the rustling of paper before his mom said anything. "So, here's the thing. Tell me what your terms are and I'll write up the offer. That way we know he isn't pulling something shady."

Henry chuckled. "Thanks Mom. I told him if I made an offer, it would be one hundred fifty thousand dollars."

"How much land is with the farm?"

"Eighty acres."

"Henry! That's an unbelievable price."

"I know. The barns are in need of repair. The house is livable. I'll certainly be asking you to come and help me decorate it. But, overall, I threw that number out never dreaming it would be accepted. I didn't even know Zander was taking it to Mr. DeWitt."

"Do you want Dad and I to come down and take a look? We'll make this offer contingent on approval from us. We'll come and look things over."

"I'd love for you to come and see it. To be honest, my heart has been hammering in my chest since I got Zander's call yesterday. First, I was in shock because I didn't actually make a verbal offer. But then, it became more of seeing myself living on the farm. Like you and Dad did. I want that for myself."

"Oh, honey. It's such a wonderful life and way to live. Especially with your job. My only wish is that it was closer to us."

He chuckled. "I know mom. But I've grown to love Glen Hollow. Even with its issues right now, I see them coming together."

"Okay. Tell me the other things you want covered in this offer. I'll write it up and email it to you. Then, your dad and I will come down this evening."

"Thanks Mom. So, I want an inspection to ensure the plumbing is okay and the electrical. I'm guessing he hasn't maintained much of anything, but I want to know what I'm getting into. And, for his sake, Mr. DeWitt is an old man. I believe him to be harmless and lonely. So, I don't expect him to repair anything at that price, I just want to know what I'm stepping into. I want a full accounting that the taxes are paid and the utilities are paid as well. That's all I want him to cover. This is an incredible deal."

"It sure sounds like it. Anything else?"

"Closing in two weeks so I can get in and start to work on it. I think he's mostly moved into an assisted living place in town here, so it shouldn't be a problem. "

"Financing?"

"I can pay cash for it. Between what I've saved and the inheritance I received from Grandpa and Grandma's estate, thanks to you, I have enough."

"Okay. I'll call you in a while and email you the offer."

"Thanks, Mom. I love you."

"I love you too, Henry."

He hung up and the hard knot that had settled in his stomach around telling his parents he'd like to buy a place here was replaced with excitement and pride. He was actually going to do this. Now he had to tell his teammates. That seemed like the harder task, and yet, he was ready. He loved them all, but he was largely raised as a farm boy, who had special operative skills both bred into him, and drilled into him in the military. It was time he began to live the way he wanted. At thirty-one, it was time.

Exiting his truck, he swaggered toward the door to the sheriff's office. A car pulled into the lot as he neared the door. He turned as Mayor Winters alighted from his truck and edged toward him.

"Morning, Henry. How's it going in there?"

Henry shook his head and shrugged. "As you'd expect, I guess. Nothing more than note gathering at this point."

He pulled the door open and held it for the mayor, then followed him inside. They entered the conference room and his eyes sought Everleigh's as he did. She smiled and nodded, and it made him feel better.

The sheriff took care of the greetings. "Mayor Rayleigh Winters, this here is Everleigh Hayes."

Everleigh stood and reached across the table to shake hands with the mayor. Henry took the opportunity to take in her slim waist and the swell of her breasts. She was put together fine. He turned his head to glance out the windows across from him, so he didn't get caught staring. Again. As he thought on it, he'd been staring at her legs this morning when she frowned at him. Clearly thinking he was a typical male chauvinist. He felt bad about that. No wonder it had set her off.

6

E verleigh closed her notebook and tucked her pen into the penholder sewn into the side. She stood, her eyes swerving to see Henry watching her, then to the mayor, who stood and chuckled.

"I think this was productive. When do you meet with Craig and the Westons?"

"I'm hoping the day after tomorrow. That's my last question of the day. Who can set up that meeting?"

Sheriff Cranford got to his feet and tucked his fingers into his front pockets. "We can make that appointment for you. I have access to Gerard via a communications unit we've provided him with. What time and where do you want to meet them?"

She looked Sheriff Cranford in the eye. "Will they come down here or do we have to travel up there?"

Sheriff Cranford shuffled back and forth on his feet, then huffed out a deep breath. "You'll likely have to go up there. But Henry here will make sure you're safe. I'll have officers close at hand should anything happen."

"Okay. Then give me a bit of time to get up there, and say nine o'clock in the morning?"

"Sounds good. I'll give you a call as soon as I confirm that will work."

She stepped past her chair, then pushed it in under the table. "Thank you. Tomorrow, I'd like to meet with the president of the town council. I'm still waiting for him to reply to my meeting request."

"Sounds good. We're all agreeable to meet with you and finalize all of this nonsense. It's time for folks to move forward."

"I agree. I'll be in touch with you both in the coming week."

She started toward the door, but Henry beat her to it and opened it for her. She offered a small smile as a thank you, then walked in front of him to the door.

He was the perfect gentleman all around. Opening doors, helping her in and out of his truck. Basically, he was doing his job. Right now her shoulders were tight and she needed to relax a bit, but she wasn't sure where to do that in this town. Normally, she'd scope out a gym or exercise facility, but it was so danged hot here, it would take her hours to cool down afterwards.

Henry jumped into his truck and his phone rang. Much to her surprise, he tapped a button on the console and said, "Hi, Mom."

"Hi, honey. I just emailed you the offer, and Dad and I will be there in about four hours."

"Fantastic. Did you call Helissa to have a room set up for you?"

"Not yet."

"I'll take care of it. See you soon. I'm in the truck now with Everleigh Hayes, the negotiator Casper sent down to settle this business with the BRR. I'll look at the offer after I drop her off at her hotel."

"Sounds good. See you later. Hello, Everleigh."

She felt deflated that he'd just drop her off and go off to do things. But then his mom said hello and it took her a few moments for it to register. "Oh, hello Ms. Delany."

Ms. Delany's laugh sounded cute and genuine. "Oh, Everleigh, call me Roxanne."

Her lips curved into a smile. "Roxanne. Hello."

"Okay. We'll see you later Henry. Everleigh, I hope to meet you while we're in town."

She eased into a smile. "I'd like that."

Henry chuckled. "Bye, Mom. See you later."

He pushed a button on his console and chuckled. "She's a great person. She's a better mom."

"That's wonderful. She said something about an offer."

He turned his head and stared into her eyes. "Yeah. I think I'm buying a farm."

"A farm? Really? And, you think?"

His cheeks tinted pink and it was handsome on him. His full lips broke into a gorgeous smile and that was even handsomer.

"My parents are phenomenal people. My dad has been an operative with GHOST for more than forty years. He's talking about retiring this year. My mom has been an attorney for nearly that same length of time. Since both of them have stressful jobs, just before I was born, they bought a hobby farm about an hour outside of Lynyrd Station, where Dad works. We spent every spare minute at the farm. By the time I was ten, Dad adjusted how many missions he went on so we could be at the farm more often. We have horses there. A few cows, chickens, and ducks. Dad just loves working his body hard to relieve the stress of his job. Mom helped out some, but she's a great cook and she kept us fed. I have one sister, Stella, who is two years younger than me. We both grew up working on the farm. I feel like it's in my blood."

"Oh, wow. That's wonderful. Are you planning to have horses?"

His right shoulder raised and lowered, and his grin was cute. "I'm not sure. Right now it needs a lot of work so it'll be a while before I can safely have any animals there."

"So you have a project on your hands."

"Yeah, I guess."

They rode in silence for a time then he softly asked, "Do you want to see it?"

She answered so quickly it startled them both. "Yes. I'd love that."

They both chuckled and he turned his truck around and headed toward the county road. He then turned down DeWitt Road. The scenery changed to one of working farms. Then, it changed again to overgrown weeds and downed fences.

"This is the beginning of the farm. As you can see, it's been left to its own devices, and I have a lot of cleaning to do." He turned onto a dirt driveway and stopped near an old barn. "This is the main barn. There are two outbuildings down that way..." He pointed to an area to her right. "And the house is up ahead." He continued to drive toward the house. It had once been white, but much of the paint had peeled and fallen. It was still straight, and the wraparound porch was something special. She could see rocking chairs and sweet tea in the evenings on something like that.

"Wow." She breathed.

7

Henry stopped his truck and inhaled a deep breath. "I'm still getting used to the fact this might be mine." The butterflies swirled around in his stomach. The excitement of his first big purchase continued to wash over him.

Everleigh chuckled. "I can only imagine. I've never owned a place of my own. I wouldn't know what to do first."

He turned to see her green eyes staring at him. Tilting his head slightly to the left he asked, "You've never owned a home? Do you rent?"

Her lips pressed into a straight line before she responded. "No. Neither. I've never owned a place and I don't even have a place of my own. I was a military brat. My parents are career military and we moved constantly. After I finished high school, I went into the military because it's all I knew. I had a penchant for negotiating and took that on as my military operational specialty. Once I left the military, I started contracting to them. Basically, they keep me busy, and my life is traveling from one job to another."

His eyes widened as he watched her pretty face fall. A sadness crept over her, and his heart hurt for her.

"I can't imagine. You don't have a home to go to between jobs?"

The right side of her mouth hiked up slightly. "No. If I have time between jobs, I either stay where I'm at for a while or move on to the next job early and see the town. If I have more time, I visit family, wherever they are."

"Does anyone in your family have a home?"

She chuckled. "My sister does. She married a great guy a couple of years ago and they have a little house in Tennessee."

"Is she happy?"

Her face lit up with the most beautiful smile. "She is. We used to talk as kids that we wanted a house. A yard. And to not have to move all the time. Plant roots. You know?"

Nodding, he replied. "Yeah. I can't imagine moving all the time. I like having a space or a place to call my own. Though I've always lived with my parents, in a barracks in the military, and now my teammates. So, this is all new for me."

Her head bobbed. He sensed her sadness in the droop of her shoulders. "Do you want to take a little tour? I can't get inside the house, but the barns are open, and I can show you some of the things I want to do here."

Her eyes brightened. "I'd love that." Her lips turned up into a smile and he liked that better than her sadness.

He jumped from his truck and hurried around to help her down. He noted her high heels again and made a mental note to not venture too far into the soft soil around the barn.

She stepped onto the ground and looked around. "It smells good here."

He chuckled. "Honeysuckle." He pointed to the honeysuckle that had managed to keep itself alive despite little or no care all this time.

"Oh. It's fragrant."

"It is. The warm air helps it release its fragrance."

"Wow, that's awesome."

He moved toward the main barn. She followed behind him and he realized he was excited to show her this place.

He lifted a lever and pushed it to the side then pulled on the large door opening the barn. He pushed the door open wide to let the light inside. The ground was mucky and he turned and held his hand out to her.

"I'm sorry, the ground is soft here. I imagine rain settled here from the cracks in the door and rotted out the walkway. It's one of many jobs I have to do here."

She chuckled. "It's okay."

She laid her hand in his and his hand tingled. He steadied her as they entered the barn.

"So, my plan right now is to have this side of the barn be all horse stalls. Depending on what I'm able to find as far as horses, that side might also be horse stalls. Then, back there is where the tack room will be located. The feed will be stored back to the right of the tack room." He pointed to the far side of the barn.

"You've been thinking about this."

"I have, but only for the past few days. My mind won't settle, and it keeps coming to me when I'm trying to rest." He shook his head. "It sounds crazy, I suppose."

"No. It doesn't. Not at all." Her head swiveled as she looked around.

He grinned. She turned to him, a gorgeous smile on her face. His pulse quickened.

Everleigh turned to look at the area inside the barn before turning back to him. "This is a great place. Where will you keep the foals?"

He snapped to attention and jerked his head toward the open barn door. "Out back in the next barn. I can show you."

He took her hand as they neared the door once again, this time, he didn't let go. She didn't try to pull away either.

As they neared the second barn he felt the ground soften under his feet and stopped. "I don't think you'll want to go any further than this with those heels on."

Her head dropped to stare at her feet as if she'd forgotten she was wearing the uncomfortable looking things.

"Yeah. Maybe next time we come out here I'll have tennis shoes on, and you can show me more of this place."

"That's a deal." He knew in that moment that he actually did want to show her more of this place.

They kept their hands clasped together as they neared his truck. In case she struggled with the terrain. At least that was his excuse. He stopped in front of the steps of the house and stared at the porch. "I've always loved a wraparound porch. My dad built one on our farm in Indiana. It's Mom's favorite place."

"I'll bet. It oozes country life and charm. A couple of rocking chairs, some hanging baskets, and it'll be picture-perfect."

He chuckled. "After some paint."

She giggled then. "Yes. After painting it."

He turned to look into her eyes. "Do you have plans later? I'm bringing my parents out here, you are welcome to join us."

"Oh. That's so nice. I'd love too, but don't want to infringe on your time with your parents."

"It's not an infringement. We'll go inside and I can show you the rest of the house. Between you and my mom, I should get some good decorating pointers."

8

Everleigh settled into Henry's truck and took another look around the house and barns as they drove from the farm. It would be a beautiful place one day. Hopefully, she'd get back this way and see it after he had it all fixed up.

That thought made her heart feel heavy and she swallowed the knot in her throat. She'd love a house of her own one day, like her sister. A place to come home to. A place to relax. Henry was about to live her dream. She was so far away from her dream it was ludicrous to even have the dream.

"How about I treat you to dinner. It's the least I can do for you carting me around and showing me your new home."

His handsome face glowed when he smiled. His stunningly beautiful blue eyes sparkled. "You don't have to buy me dinner. I'm getting paid to cart you around."

Ouch. Her stomach twisted and her cheeks felt as though they'd caught fire.

"I'm aware that I'm a job. I was trying to be nice."

His brows bunched slightly. "I didn't mean to hurt your feelings. It's just that you don't owe me anything."

"I don't think I owe you anything. I was simply inviting you..." She huffed out a breath. "Never mind."

He cleared his throat. "How about we go to Porter's Steakhouse and have an early dinner. Then, I'll take you to the hotel so you can change before we head over to meet my parents."

"Without sounding like I'm trying to be difficult, can we go to the hotel first? I'd love to put on some comfortable clothes and get my feet out of these heels."

He grinned and a ribbon of excitement twirled in her belly. "Deal."

He turned the truck toward the Homeland Guest House. She turned to him and smiled. "Do you mind telling me about Glen Hollow? Where everything is. What you like? Places you enjoy?"

His chuckle was comforting, a sigh escaped her lungs, and her shoulders began to relax.

"Sure, this road is DeWitt Road. It's named after the man I'm buying my farm from. His family settled here close to one hundred years ago. He and his wife built the farm I'm buying. We can turn right, out of the driveway, and that will turn into First Street where a good many businesses are located. If we turn left, it will take us past where my colleagues and I live now. It used to be an old sewing factory but our company, GHOST, converted it last year into living, working, work out quarters. We call it the HOG. Home. Office. Garage."

His smile spread across his face, and she saw the hint of a dimple on his right cheek.

She laughed. "That makes perfect sense."

His head bobbed. "Right now, we're in the middle of a

renovation on the second floor of the HOG. Tate, our leader, and his wife, Lara, who by the way makes the best cookies you'll ever eat, and has a little bakery on First Street, Lara's Delights, just announced they're expecting a baby in January. So, they're planning on moving upstairs and there will be room for more team members and their children in the future."

"Wow. That's wonderful. How many of your teammates are married?"

"Tate and Lara. Aidyn married Elena. They moved back to Indiana though. Elena lived up on the mountain and was the brewer of the elixir. Aidyn killed Craig's father, the former president. It wasn't safe for them to stay. But they have a baby now, Teagan, a little girl. And Spencer and Kenna married last week."

"Okay. So more babies could be coming sooner rather than later?"

He shrugged. "I suppose so."

"Is that all of you then?"

"No. Addie, Adelaide Masters, and her cousins, Maya Sager, and her twin brother Myles Sager, live there. And, of course me. But I'll be moving on soon.

"There are a lot of you there. Does that get hectic?"

He laughed and she loved the sound of his deep, throaty laugh. "Sometimes. But the HOG is big. And, we've all grown up with each other our entire lives. Our parents, one or the other and in Myles and Maya's case, both parents, all work for GHOST. We've been together since birth. So, it's the usual for us."

"Your house is going to feel very quiet."

She saw his Adam's apple bob as he swallowed. "I know."

"Does that worry you?"

He turned and stared into her eyes a moment, then turned to watch the road. "A little. I can always go to the HOG and stay if I need to or want to. They can always come out by me. We're close. I'm not breaking up with them or leaving them. Just like when I was little, my parents whisked my sister and I away to our farm every chance they got. So, I guess, I'm used to straddling both worlds."

He turned the truck into the parking lot of the Homeland Guest House. She hesitated before asking, "Did you want to come in while I change?"

He grinned. "I need to look this offer over my mom emailed. I can do that out here."

"Or at the desk in the lobby." She smiled at him, to ease the awkwardness of the moment.

"Or the desk in the lobby." He chuckled.

He opened her door and they walked side by side to the front door. Inside, she pointed to the little office space set up in the corner. "I'll be down soon."

"Take your time." He moved off to the desk and she hesitated briefly as she watched his stride. Confident. Sure of himself. Yet, she felt sorry for him in some way. Like he was all alone.

Letting out a breath, she went to the elevator and stepped inside.

As she entered her room, she let her shoulders slump against the door, her back pressed tightly to it. She let her head rest on the door as well and focused on regular breathing and relaxation. It was only four o'clock, but it had been a full day already. Still, she was grateful to spend time with Henry. She wouldn't be alone this evening, which made her feel so much better than she had earlier. Life on the road sucked most times.

9

Henry sent his mom an email. Then he typed out an email to Zander Zamora.

"My mom wrote up an Offer to Purchase for the DeWitt farm. I have attached it to this email. My parents are coming to town tonight and would like to see the farm. Will you be available to let us inside?"

He sent that off and closed his laptop. Rotating his head on his shoulders he wondered when he'd stop bouncing between excitement and worry. Sometimes he was so danged excited he could barely sit. Then others, he wondered how he'd do it all by himself. It was taking its toll on him. He hadn't slept in a couple of days because his brain kept rolling through all he had to do for the farm to get it up and running, and the stress settled in his shoulders and back.

He stood and stretched his back, arching back as far as he could and held until his muscles felt better.

Tucking his laptop into its case, he hefted the strap over his shoulder, and walked to the bank of windows in the waiting area of the lobby. This place was nice. He liked the old and new they'd mixed in the decorating. He didn't know much about that kind of stuff. He was going to lean heavy on his mom for that. At least she was good at it.

"I'm all set if you are."

He spun around at the sound of Everleigh's voice. "I am."

He held his hand out in front of him for her to precede him through the door.

She wore nice jeans, tan sneakers, and a white button-up blouse with little detailing on the collar. She looked casual but not too casual. Actually, she looked fantastic.

He hurried to the door of his truck and opened it for her. Her lips parted in the most beautiful smile he'd seen in years. It reminded him of sparkling diamonds. Her lips shined where she'd added some gloss and he noticed the hint of a dimple on her right cheek.

She jumped up into his truck with ease and he took a few deep breaths as he strode around his truck to get in. He deposited his laptop in the backseat before starting the truck.

"I take it you haven't been to Porters."

Her cheeks tinted a soft pink and her soft smile hinted at a bit of shyness. "No. I have only been to the sheriff's department and your new farm besides the hotel."

"Okay. So, how about this?" He looked at his watch. "It's nearly four-thirty, which is a little early for Porters. So, to give them until five o'clock, how about I show you around town?"

"I'd love that." Her eyes settled on his and he was struck breathless.

He stopped his truck at the exit and pointed across the street.

"So, just across the street here is Divine Designs.

Shianne Brown owns that store. She's Lara's best friend. She sells clothing, dresses, all that stuff."

"I'll have to stop in while I'm here."

Turning left from the parking lot, he pointed to the grocery store. "That's Paxton's. The only grocery in town. Next to Paxton's is Flynn's gas station. And next to Flynn's is the courthouse. Across from the courthouse is Homemade in the Hollow."

"Oh, I ordered supper from there last night. They delivered."

"They have good food."

She laughed. "And a lot of it. I couldn't finish my order."

He chuckled and turned onto First Street. "This is where the majority of the businesses are. So first on the right is the Paper Trail. That's Kenna's business."

"Kenna married one of your teammates, right?"

"Yes. Spencer."

"Next to Paper Trail is Smith Squared, a law office. Next to them is Stackable Reads, the bookstore, and library. Then Lara's Delights..."

"The best cookies I'll ever eat!"

He laughed. "Yes. I promise you that." He glanced at her smiling face and his heartbeat stuttered.

"What's Chestnut Grove? Looks to be furniture."

"Yes, it's furniture. Across the street to the left is Hairy Beards, the barber."

She burst out laughing. "Really?"

"He's a German man with a strong accent and a sense of humor you won't forget."

"Okay." Her eyes sparkled.

"Then Lady Liberty, another law office. Next to them is Bloomin' Lovely, the flower shop and Squeaky Clean the laundromat. There are other businesses here and there, but this is the heart of Glen Hollow."

"Okay. It's a great little town. Everything is so clean. I can see why you like it here."

"The people here are very nice too. It's a slower pace here, and now that much of the trouble from the BRR has stopped, it's settling in to be a great place to raise a family."

She turned to look at him. He saw her swallow. She nodded. "I can see that." She filled her lungs with air and slowly let it out and he wondered why that affected her.

He liked the mood better a few minutes ago, so he turned onto the county road and headed toward Porter's. "See that tree right there? The big one?"

"Yep."

"When Aidyn and Elena were still getting to know each other, he wasn't allowed anywhere near the mountain or the BRR in general. But he saw Elena one night and I think he fell in love with her right then and there. She wasn't allowed to come down to town. But, at the base of the tree in all those plants, she'd leave him a basket with notes tucked inside, and he'd come and get it and leave her notes and gifts in return. One of the gifts he left her was Lara's cookies."

He laughed.

Everleigh's head whipped around and she stared at him. "Really?"

"Really."

She laughed too. "Wow, what a cool story they have to tell their kids."

He cocked his head to the side and nodded. "I guess they do."

He pulled into Porter's. "We can eat inside or outside. Which do you prefer?"

"How about outside. The heat has lifted a bit."

"Sounds good." They walked into Porter's together, he held his hand at the small of her back and her perfume filled his nostrils. She smelled fresh and clean and slightly citrusy. It was a great smell.

10

His hand pressed slightly against the small of her back and her pulse quickened. It had been years, literally years, since she'd been on a date. Not that this was a date, but it sort of felt like one. She'd missed this. Dating. Feeling like you wanted to spend time with someone else. He made her not feel so lonely. He was kind. And, handsome. And, gentlemanly. He was so much.

The hostess brought them through the restaurant and out the back door to a cute patio area that overlooked the woods. It was peaceful and there was only one other couple seated at a table. It felt semi-private.

He held her chair out and she brushed his arm slightly as she sat. He smelled so good. She'd noticed him this morning and the way he smelled. Musky and spicy. Such a manly smell and he was definitely all man.

As he sat across from her, her eyes again landed on the way his t-shirt stretched across his biceps. It stretched across his chest too. Her hand shook slightly as she picked up her glass of water and sipped.

The hostess handed them each their menus and walked away.

"What have you had here that's good?"

He grinned. "I always eat steak. They have the best steaks here, and a lot of it. Just like Homemade in the Hollow, you'll get plenty to eat here."

She chuckled and silently chastised herself for letting her thoughts go to a date. To think Henry would be interested in her in that way was foolish. As soon as negotiations were over, she'd be gone. He was buying a farm here and talking about raising a family. They were in different places.

"Did Carson Simek, the town board president, call to confirm your appointment for tomorrow?"

"Oh, I'm glad you asked. Yes, I'm meeting him at the town hall at eight-thirty tomorrow morning. Will that work for you? If not, I can go myself."

He laughed and she couldn't stop staring at him. "Whatever you are doing is what I'm doing."

Heat flew up from her core. Her chest burned, then her neck, and finally her cheeks. Her hair even prickled, and she resisted the urge to fan herself. She hadn't had a reaction to anyone like this, well, ever. She'd dated a couple handsome men back in the day. She never burned up at the slightest smile.

A waitress stopped at their table. "Can I get you two something to drink?"

"Oh." She glanced at Henry waiting to see what he was going to order.

He smiled at her. Oh, it was drool worthy too. "I'm on duty, but please feel free to have a drink if you like."

No way was she going to have alcohol in his presence.

She had trouble controlling her emotions sober. "I'd like an iced tea, please."

"Sweet tea, hon?"

"Yes, sweet tea."

"And how about you, handsome." The waitress practically drooled.

Henry chuckled, his eyes darted to hers before he responded. "I'll have sweet tea also."

"You got it." The waitress hustled off and Henry chuckled again.

"I love how they talk to you here. Hon, handsome, sugar, it's all so endearing."

She giggled. "It is. I've always loved the south for that reason."

The waitress brought their teas, then took their orders before hustling off once again.

Henry looked across the table and stared into her eyes. "Tell me why you went into negotiating."

"I always had a penchant for it, I guess. My mom used to say I negotiated my way out of her womb."

He laughed and it was spectacular.

"I guess that means you were born to it."

"I guess it does. Did you always want to be a special operative?"

"I didn't know anything else. Except farming. But, when we were kids, Tate and the group, we always played special ops games. We'd have our parents come up with a scenario, and we'd play it out. It's what I always expected to do."

"Your mom's an attorney, you never wanted to go into law?"

His handsome face scrunched slightly. Even that was sexy. "Oh, good lord no. Too awful."

"But you deal with the criminal element all the time."

"But, on this side of the law, so to speak, I can make sure they don't continue to be criminals."

"True." She sipped at her tea. "What does your sister do for a living?"

"She's an attorney and living in Indianapolis. She works in private practice in real estate law."

"Like your mom?"

His right shoulder rose and fell. "Mom was largely a business attorney. Real estate was a small part of what she did. But, she's excellent at both."

"Wow, your parents must be so proud of you both."

His grin was adorable. The pink in his cheeks was too. "They are. I'm sure your parents are proud of you as well."

"I'm sure they are in their way. My sister, Marina, is a veterinarian in Tennessee."

His brows furrowed slightly. "Why do you say in their own way?"

She smiled at him. He was empathetic and concerned. How refreshing. "My parents are very driven. They don't show emotion easily and seldom tell us they're proud of us. My dad thinks that builds character."

His lips formed a straight line. The waitress brought their meals and her eyes rounded at the size of the steak on his plate.

"Oh my. You weren't kidding."

He grinned and shook his head. "Nope."

Her chicken was crispy and delicious. But she envied Henry's steak. It smelled amazing.

Their meal was nearly over when his phone rang. "Excuse me, please."

He stood and exited the patio to the backyard area.

She watched his face as he talked. He smiled a lot,

laughed a couple of times then pocketed his phone. He entered through the back door and she noted how he filled the room. He was impressive.

"My parents are here. They're at the HOG now. When we're finished with dinner, we'll meet them at the farm."

"Okay. I'll bet they're so excited for you."

He chuckled. "They are."

She felt a bit of envy. What it must be like to be close to your parents. She had no idea. She saw her parents, maybe a week every other year or so.

11

H enry and Everleigh pulled into the driveway of his farm. Yes, it was sinking in that this was his farm. His farm!

His eyes scanned the area and didn't see his dad's truck or his mom's SUV. He parked and glanced at Everleigh. "Ready?"

She chuckled. "I'm ready. Are you?"

Laughter bubbled up in his belly. "Gotta be honest. I'm fucking excited right now."

She laughed with him. He looked into her eyes, her lips turned up into a gorgeous smile. "I'm excited for you. This is tremendous."

He exited the truck and hustled around the front to help Everleigh down. She took his hand as she stepped down, and he squeezed her fingers. "Thank you for coming back here tonight."

"Thank you for inviting me. I didn't want to spend the entire evening alone."

"I'll bet you have a lot of lonely nights on the road."

Her smile didn't reach her eyes when she replied. "Yeah."

He turned so they were toe to toe. "You know, I asked why you went into negotiating, but I failed to ask if you always wanted to do it. Did you? Always want to be a negotiator?"

Her head tilted back so their eyes met. "My parents decided for me."

"So, that's a no."

"I don't know what it is exactly."

He nodded his head and turned toward the house. Everleigh turned with him, and they stared at the tired old house in need of repair together in silence. It was comfortable though, and he'd never quite felt that before.

After a long while, Everleigh softly said, "If you repaint the house white, you can paint the trim black. Black rocking chairs on the porch, two sets of them." She pointed. "Two there with a little table in between." She moved her hand to the other side of the porch. "And two over there. You can watch the horses in the pasture on the first and the foals in the pasture on the second."

He looked down into her smiling face and his lips broke open into a large smile. "That's a fantastic idea."

"Honeysuckle in mason jars on each table will bring the aroma up to the house."

He put his arm around her shoulders and squeezed her to his body. "That's a great idea."

She giggled lightly. The sound of his dad's truck approaching drowned her out, and they turned to face the oncoming vehicle.

He chuckled. "Here we go."

Her arm wrapped around his waist from the back, and

she squeezed him tightly, then dropped her arm. Reassurance. She was reassuring him. His heart swelled.

He took her hand as he walked toward his parents. His mom stepped to him and wrapped him in a big hug. His mom's hugs had a way of soothing him when he was younger. It was the same now as he embarked on this big purchase.

His dad clapped him on the back and husked, "Don't go hogging him, Luna."

His mom giggled and stepped back. His dad wrapped him in a bear hug, and he heard his mom introduce herself to Everleigh.

His dad whispered, "It's so nice to see you, son."

"It's great to see you, Dad."

He stepped back and looked at Everleigh. "Everleigh, this is my dad, Hawk. I see you've met my mom, Roxanne."

"Yes. It's nice to meet you Mr. De..."

"Hawk. Just Hawk. It's nice to meet you too, Everleigh."

"Hawk." Her cheeks turned an adorable shade of pink.

Zander's car finally rolled up the driveway, and he grinned and swallowed. It was go time.

Zander made his way to them and introduced himself. "What do you want to see first, the house or the barns?"

He glanced down at his mom. "House please." She glanced at him and smiled.

Zander walked ahead of them, he held his hand out to Everleigh to precede him. His mom stepped in with Everleigh and his dad grabbed his nape and squeezed affectionately.

"Are you excited about this, Henry?"

He laughed. "I'm so fucking excited, Dad. It's been back and forth really, excitement and fear but the past few hours, it's been pure excitement."

His dad chuckled. "Good."

They climbed the steps to the porch and Zander unlocked the door. He turned and looked out at the pasture area where Everleigh had pointed earlier. He could see the horses in the pasture from this spot.

His eyes sought hers and she grinned and nodded.

They stepped back in time when they entered the house. Everyone stood in a state of bewildered silence. "Mr. DeWitt didn't believe in updating the furniture or the home. Look at the woodwork, it's all original." Zander commented.

His mom laid her hand on the newel post at the bottom of the stairs and tried to shake it. It stood firm against her motions, and she exclaimed, "Wow."

He stepped forward into the living room and stared at the antique furniture. "Look at all of the antiques."

Zander piped up then. "He says you can purchase whatever you want. He obviously has no need for it. His daughter took everything she wanted already, so what's in here is available."

"Oh, Henry, this is fantastic." His mom sighed. She ran her hand over an antique sofa. She looked across the room at the other antique pieces. Henry turned to see his dad's eyes watching his mom and he chuckled. Mom and Dad were going to be going home with some antiques.

Zander continued on, "Let's go see the kitchen."

Henry glanced at Everleigh and saw her watching his mom. She turned her face up to him and smiled. "I think she approves." Her smile was radiant and his excitement changed to something different.

His dad exited with Zander and his mom lingered. Henry took Everleigh's hand and led her to the kitchen, suddenly he felt entirely different about a few things. Thoughts swirled through his head. The farm. The work. The HOG. Everleigh. His parents. Did he want this furniture? What would he work on first? So much.

12

Everleigh shifted as she sat in Henry's truck. "You didn't tell me your mom is gorgeous."

He glanced at her then back to the road. His right shoulder hitched up then dropped. "I guess she's just my mom. I mean, I know she's beautiful, but to tell others that seems weird."

She chuckled. "I suppose it does. But she is absolutely stunning."

"I'll let her know you think so."

"Oh, god no. Don't do that. That would seem weird."

He laughed and she stared at him. His smile was stunning. When he laughed he didn't look as broody as usual.

"If you want to join us at the HOG, you're more than welcome."

She turned to face the windshield. "I appreciate it. And maybe there will be another day you'll invite me. But I really need to prepare for meeting Carson Simek tomorrow. I'd love to meet everyone, but I also have to make sure I'm ready for work."

"I understand. I just wanted you to know you're welcome."

"Thank you."

Her mind wandered to all they'd done today. "How many pieces of furniture are your parents going home with?"

He threw his head back and laughed. "I was thinking about that. My dad was eyeing my mom and she was eyeing up piece after piece. Thing is, she has a great eye for that stuff and she'll freshen it up and either use it at the farm or sell it."

"That's a great skill to have."

"Have you ever refinished furniture?"

Her heart felt heavy, like a rock dropping down a well. "No. My parents weren't into that sort of thing. Usually, we used whatever furniture was available on base."

"I can't imagine. So much of who I am is wrapped up in living in a home with people I love."

She turned her head toward him. "You're fortunate. So many people wish for a life like that."

They drove in silence for a bit. "Do you? Wish for a life like that?"

Tears rushed to her eyes and she blinked furiously to dry them. Taking a cleansing breath, she responded, "Yeah. I do. I'm going to have to decide what to do for a living before that can ever happen though."

"Ah, yes. That's the rub isn't it?"

"Yes. I suppose it is."

Henry pulled into the parking lot at the hotel and she sucked in enough air to fill her lungs. "Thank you for the great evening. I enjoyed seeing your new place. And meeting your parents."

"I'm glad you joined us. I'll be here a little after eight in the morning to make sure you arrive on time for your meeting with Simek."

"Thank you. Have a great night."

Henry started to open his door and she touched his arm. "Don't bother. I can manage. Thank you. See you in the morning."

Before she did something stupid like cry, she opened her door and jumped from the truck. She waved and smiled, then turned and hurried into the hotel. The lobby was blissfully empty, and she hustled to the elevator and sighed when it opened quickly.

Exiting on her floor she wasted no time hurrying to her door. Once inside, she let the tears fall for about five minutes. Then, she splashed water on her face in the bathroom, dabbed her face dry on the hand towel, looked at herself in the mirror and said out loud, "Get a grip. Get to work. Stop being a crybaby."

It was something her father had told her over and over all her life. Leaving the bathroom, she went straight to her desk and opened her computer. She read over her notes from her meeting today, edited typos, and created a list of questions to ask Carson Simek tomorrow. Then, she'd prepare to meet the infamous Craig Howard. After meeting with Craig, she'd pull together an agreement for all of the parties to look over and from there, tweaks and edits would take place. But, she'd likely be gone by late next week.

That thought made her sadder than she'd felt before. She'd leave Glen Hollow. And Henry. She liked him. He was solid and sure and strong. Mostly, she enjoyed talking to him. He knew what he wanted and that felt like a security she'd never known. Her entire life was about packing and moving to the next place. Not really knowing what she wanted, but doing what she had to.

What did she want? That was the golden question, that to this day had eluded her.

Her phone chimed and she picked it off the table and saw a text from her sister, Marina.

"What are you doing? Can you talk?"

Her fingers flew across the keyboard on her phone screen. "Yes, I can talk."

"Calling you right now."

She took a couple of deep breaths and waited for Marina to call her. Her phone rang and she answered it before the first ring stopped.

"Hey. How are you?"

Her sister's sing-song voice laughed. "Wow, you had your phone in your hand."

"Well, you did just text me."

"Right. Okay, so we have news."

"Okay. I can't wait to hear it."

"You're going to be an aunty."

Her heartbeat increased as if she'd just run a mile. "Really? Oh, my god. Oh, my god. I can't believe it. Congratulations."

Marina laughed. "I'm so excited. I want you to be here when he or she is born. Do you think you'll be able to manage that?"

"I'll do my absolute best. I promise."

"I'm going to hold you to it. I called Mom and Dad and they barely said congratulations. Dad started in about how much work kids are and Mom said, 'I hope it's just like you.' I don't even know if that's good or bad."

"Aww, well, from my point of view, it's good. So, so good."

"Thank you, Ev. I miss you like crazy."

And then, tears fell. "I miss you too." And they fell harder.

"What's going on? Are you alright?"

She sniffed, then reached over to the tissue box and pulled a tissue from it and dabbed at her eyes. "I guess I'm feeling lonely."

"Oh, honey. Come here. You can stay with us. Come here to me."

"I'm in the middle of a job right now. And, I met someone."

"Oh. I need to hear."

Everleigh swallowed. "He's actually my bodyguard. Sort of. I have protection for this job because one of the parties is unpredictable. He's so damned handsome Mar. He's awesome. He's got the biggest heart. He has a great family. He's smart. He's stable, solid, and knows what he wants. He's..."

Marina laughed. "He's the bomb! Send me a picture."

"I don't have one. I'll take one though. I only met him this morning. But we've spent the entire day together. He just bought a farm and he took me there and showed me. His parents came to see it. We had dinner. We talked. Oh, Marina, he's so..."

"Ev? Are you ready to settle down?"

"Oh my god. Mar, I only met him today. Hardly planning on settling down."

"I mean, are YOU ready to settle down? If he's buying farms and planning a life in one spot, do you want to get involved with someone who won't understand that you have to go off to work? That you might not be home for weeks? Or, are you ready to change your career?"

"I don't know. I'm just feeling...blue I guess."

13

Henry closed the door to his parents' room at the HOG. While they settled in, he'd go outside and get a fire ready in the firepit.

Striding through the kitchen, Tate called out, "Henry?"

Turning on his heel, he faced Tate as he crossed toward him.

"How did it go today with the sheriff and the mayor?"

"I think it went well. They were both very pointed in their comments to Everleigh's questions. She asked probing questions to make sure they weren't playing games with her or the BRR. No ulterior motives or ill intent. They stated their case."

Tate nodded. "And tomorrow she meets with the town council president, Carson Simek?"

He grinned. "Yes. And the following day is when she finally meets Craig."

"How do you think that will go?"

Henry shrugged. "For her part, I think she's preparing. I've tried explaining that Craig is unpredictable. She accepts that he is, but honestly, I don't think she has a clue as to what she's dealing with. She's used to people coming to the table to negotiate. Craig doesn't want to negotiate, he wants things as they were."

Tate nodded. "That's a fact."

Henry's parents entered the kitchen. "Hi, Tate!" His mom greeted.

Tate turned and leaned over to hug Henry's mom. His dad shook Tate's hand and slapped him on the back. "How is it running your own team?"

Tate chuckled. "It's been good. This team is like working with my siblings, so it's same as always I guess. I just take more phone calls now."

His dad laughed. "Yep, that's the bad part of running a team. I'd much rather just be out there getting dirty." His dad grinned. "Also, we understand congratulations are in order."

Tate laughed. "Thank you. We're very excited."

His mom smiled. "Do you know what you're having yet?"

Shaking his head, "Not yet. I guess we have another month or two to wait for that news."

His mom's smile was genuine. "That's right. Maybe by the time Henry moves, you'll know and we'll all celebrate together."

Henry's eyes widened. He hadn't told his parents that his teammates didn't know anything yet. His eyes slowly slid to Tate's and his heartbeat raced. "I guess I have something to tell you all."

His mom gasped. "I'm so sorry. I thought you'd told them."

He shook his head and put his arm around his mom's shoulders. Easy to do, she was much shorter than him.

"It's alright. To be honest, I've been struggling to figure out how to bring it up. So, this is as good a way as any."

He turned to Tate. "I bought a farm. Or I should say, I'm buying a farm. The DeWitt Farm, not far from here. I've actually clocked it and it's less than two miles from here. It's a project and in need of repair. It'll be awhile before I actually move into it, but..." He swallowed as he saw Tate swallow emotion. His breathing stuttered and he let out a breath. "I'm fucking stoked, Tate." He motioned to his parents. "It's how I grew up. Farming and special ops. Working with Dad out on the farm with the animals. It was inevitable that I'd buy one. I saw this farm the other day and spoke to the realtor and he pulled a fast one and told Mr. DeWitt what I was thinking about offering for it and Mr. DeWitt accepted. Mom wrote the offer up today. We just came from looking at it."

Tate stepped toward him and wrapped him in a hug. "Congratulations, buddy. I'm happy for you." Tate stepped back. "I'm surprised, but happy. I didn't know you liked it here enough to plant roots."

Henry shook his head. "You know, this town has just grown on me."

Tate laughed. "Me too. So what's the plan moving forward?"

Henry laughed, "Well for tonight, I thought we could have a fire outside and sit around and chat. I guess it'll be a good time to tell everyone what's happening. Then, tomorrow I'll call the realtor and set up a time you can all come out and see it. Besides, I think Mom found some furniture she wants there."

His mom laughed. "Dad told me to curb my enthusiasm. And, I'm trying, but it's a treasure trove of goodies."

Tate chuckled. "Don't tell my mom. She'll bring a moving truck down and fill it full."

"Oh, my God, that's a great idea."

His dad shook his head. "No. Luna, no. Please, don't fill our shed with furniture."

His mom stood on her toes and kissed her father's cheek. "I'll share it with Sophie, Yvette, Bridget, and Isi. I promise."

She turned and skipped off to the bedroom and his dad shook his head. He looked at Tate, "Better plan on a barrage of women coming soon."

Tate laughed. "It'll be good to see everyone. And, I'd love to see my parents again."

Hawk groaned and Henry laughed. This could be great fun. Also, it would be good to get them all planning on working in the house. Painting, cleaning, fixing. He'd make it an all-out GHOST project.

Tate chuckled as he left the room and Henry turned to his dad. "Sorry, Dad. But not really that much."

His dad circled his shoulders with a big beefy arm. "It's all good, Henry. This makes your mom happy, and I love her most when she's happy. Plus, I suspect you'll get some benefit out of having them all help you clean the place out."

He threw his head back and laughed. "I was just thinking that same thing."

His dad squeezed his shoulders and stepped back. "What were you off to do?"

"Oh, build a fire. Want to join me?"

"I'd love to. It's one of my specialties you know."

Laughing, Henry responded, "Oh, I'm aware. It's who I learned it from. Come on out and we'll set up the chairs and get the fire going. We can have a beer or two while we wait for the others to join us."

His dad chuckled. "That sounds like a plan."

14

Everleigh jotted questions she wanted to ask Carson Simek, then closed her notebook and tucked it into her laptop case. She hefted the strap over her shoulder and exited her room. She was excited to get to the meeting with Simek. But she was more excited to see Henry. Despite her sister's cautions to the contrary. Stepping off the elevator she sauntered into the breakfast area and made herself a bowl of oatmeal and picked up a ripe banana. Filling a cup of coffee, she set them all on the table closest to the window looking out over the woods in the back.

There were a couple of horses playing in a paddock not far away. Youngsters, jumping around and teasing each other. She laughed out loud as she watched them. A grown horse stepped between the playing foals, and they stopped jumping at each other and fell in line alongside her.

She wondered what Henry's horses would look like. She could imagine sitting on that generous wraparound porch on a warm summer evening watching them play.

She'd always thought horses were graceful and sleek animals. Had her childhood been one like Henry's, she'd have had a horse growing up. Marina would have too.

"Looks like you're ready for the day."

She swiveled her head toward him at the sound of his voice. His deep, throaty, sexy voice. He looked...handsome. He wore black jeans, a black three button placket shirt, the sleeves stretched tightly around his biceps. His deep blue eyes set against the black eyelashes was picture worthy.

She blinked and masked her sigh. "I am. Just let me toss my empty bowl."

Standing, her knees shook slightly as she scrambled to the garbage can to toss her trash. Laying the tray on top of the can, she squirted hand sanitizer from the bottle hanging on the wall above the can. She hurried to her table and picked her laptop off the chair back and slung it over her shoulder as she neared him. She'd been acutely aware that his eyes followed her everywhere she went. She'd been watching him from the corner of her eye as well.

As he escorted her to his truck, she felt his hand press lightly at the small of her back and butterflies spun in her tummy. When he leaned forward to open the door for her the fresh scent of his aftershave circled around her, and she closed her eyes to memorize the scent. It was slightly intoxicating.

Moving toward the exit, she remembered his parents. "Did you have a nice night?"

His grin showed that dimple in his right cheek and she stared at the dazzling little divot. How could something like that make him sexier? She didn't know, but dammit, it did.

"We had a nice time. My mom let it slip that I'd bought the farm..." He turned and looked into her eyes. "So to speak." He chuckled, "So my entire company now knows. And the other women are planning a trip down to pick up the furniture inside."

Her stomach grew hot and heavy at the mention of the other women. It was a direct reminder that she didn't know anything about Henry, like, did he have a girlfriend? More than one?

Her voice sounded hoarse when she asked, "How many other women are you talking about?"

She cleared the lump in her throat and stared as he grinned again. "I guess four. I'm not sure if Elena will come with them, since it's safer for her here now. But, with the new baby, I doubt she'd make the trip."

"Four. Wow. They could have that place cleaned out in no time."

He threw his head back and laughed. "That's what my dad said."

Turning toward the windshield and the road, she practiced even breathing to settle her racing heart and her erratic breathing. Why this conversation had her so mixed up was bewildering.

Henry seemed oblivious. "Mom said Bridget, that's Aiden's mom. I told you about Aiden, right?"

"Yes."

"Okay. Mom said Bridget would have a field day out at the farm. Her style is more old-fashioned than the others. Isi and Josh, their home is more Spanish in style. Sophie and Gaige, that's my boss and Tate's parents, their style is more modern. Yvette and Wyatt, that's Spencer's parents, they have a few pieces of antique furniture in their house, but not many. So, she'll likely enjoy the shopping."

So these were all the parents of his teammates. She felt a slight relief at finding out he didn't mean anyone he was connected to. Other than his mom of course. But no one of a girlfriend capacity. Of course, it didn't matter, because she'd be moving on soon.

He turned the truck into a parking lot. The silver lettering on the outside of the building said "Town Hall". Under it in smaller letters, "Glen Hollow, KY". The building was brick, and square and not nearly as quaint as she expected.

As she stared at the building, Henry left the vehicle and strode around the front of the truck. He helped her from the truck, her hand in his. Butterflies awoke in her belly, and she sighed.

She stepped into the building and was mildly surprised that the inside didn't match the outside. The square brick building with no personality on the outside warmly greeted her with country touches, flowers in mason jars on the counter above the receptionist. Photographs on the walls depicted the history of Glen Hollow.

"Good morning. May I help you?" The receptionist greeted.

"Good morning. Everleigh Hayes and Henry Delany here to see Mr. Simek."

"I'll let him know you're here."

The kindly lady stood and with much effort, limped to a door alongside her desk and poked her head inside. "Ms. Hayes and Mr. Delany are here to see you."

Everleigh watched the woman limp back to the desk, her back seemed too stiff to make movement easy and the limp suggested a hip issue. She confirmed just that as she sat down behind the desk once again.

"I have arthritis and need a hip replacement. That's coming in a month or so. It seems silly to say I'm looking forward to it, but all I've heard from others is the pain is less than I'm in now. So, it's welcome."

"Good luck with your surgery. I've heard that as well." Everleigh smiled at the poor lady.

"Good."

The door next to the desk opened and a man stepped out and faced her. He was balding, had a mustache and a bit of a beer belly. But he was impeccably dressed in a nice suit and clean shoes.

"Ms. Hayes and Mr. Delany. Please come in."

15

A nother day spent listening to Everleigh question the various members of the Town Council. First up was Simek. After Simek, he insisted she talk to a couple of the other members. She dutifully listened to their concerns and took notes. He admired her dedication to listening to the little gripes and complaints without commenting on how petty they were.

She stood and stretched, her eyes searching for his. Throughout the day they'd stared across the room. Grinned, nodded periodically. He enjoyed silently communicating with her.

She pushed in her chair, shook hands with whoever this council member was, he'd lost track of them all. He felt like a fixture in the corner and his muscles ached to get on the farm.

Everleigh stepped toward him, a sweet smile on her face. "How about that for a day?"

Shaking his head, "I don't know how you do it. Some of these guys are just downright petty."

Her throat constricted as she swallowed and her smile

faded, which made him sad. "I know. It usually goes this way when the wound has been festering for a long time. Neither side wants to let anything go. I suspect tomorrow's meeting will be filled with petty complaints too."

"Ugh," His stomach dropped. It would be a long day indeed. At this point, Craig could go to hell for all he'd done here. For him to have any petty arguments was bullshit.

Henry glanced at his watch, "Do you have plans for this evening?"

His heartbeat quickened as he waited for her to respond. "I don't. How about you?"

"Nope. Why don't you join my parents and I for dinner? I promised to take them to Porters. Of course, that means we'll have eaten there two nights in a row. Are you up for it?"

She chuckled. "I am. It was great last night. But I don't want to take up your time with your parents."

He laughed and shook his head. "Don't worry about that. They liked you." He leaned in, "And so do I."

Her eyes snapped to his. Her lips formed the smile to beat all smiles. "I like you too." Her cheeks turned a pretty shade of pink and his stomach fluttered.

He held his hand out for her to precede him from this stifling room. He followed closely behind her, careful not to let his eyes wander to her ass, but damn if that wasn't where he wanted to look.

The fresh air hit him square in the face as they left the building they'd sat in for the past six hours. He let his hand lay in the small of her back and a thrill ran through his body when she tilted her head up and smiled at him. He grinned and inwardly celebrated just being near her once again.

Once he'd pulled them from the parking lot he asked, "Do you want to go to the hotel and change?"

"Yes, please. What time are you planning on having dinner?"

He shrugged his right shoulder, "I believe my mom said six. That will give you a couple of hours to relax and let the day fall away."

She sighed, "That sounds lovely."

He navigated a corner. "If this job sits so heavy on your shoulders, why don't you do something else?"

She chuckled, "My sister kind of said the same thing to me last night. The quick answer is I don't know what I'd like to do. I've always been told this was my path and wasn't allowed to consider anything else."

He swallowed the dry lump of irritation in his throat. How could her parents not encourage her to do what she liked? "What do you like to do. Say, for fun?"

Her cheeks turned a deep pink and her eyes pointed to her shoes. "I don't know how to answer that. My life is work, then more work."

He quickly turned the truck into a parking lot and swung around to head out to the road in the direction they'd come from.

"What's going on?"

"I want to show you some things in town."

He pulled into the parking lot of Blooming Lovely, the flower shop in town. He jumped from the vehicle and mentally shook off the irritation he felt at her parents. As he helped her down from his truck, he held her hand and tugged her lightly into the store. Inside, the smell of various flowers enveloped them. Mixed with the cool air, it felt to him a bit cloying, but he wanted to see if she liked plants and flowers.

"What are you looking for in here?" She whispered.

"To be honest, I wondered if you liked it in here. Do you like flowers and plants?"

She shrugged. "I guess. I mean they're pretty. But I don't know a thing about them."

"But do you want to learn?"

Her head tilted and her slim brows furrowed slightly. "Not really."

He grinned. "That's a start."

Her head shook but she said nothing. She turned and looked at the flowers on display, slowly sidling along the rows. "This one's pretty."

"What is it?" He questioned.

Her slender shoulders shrugged once more. "I don't know." Lifting a tag from the side of the flower she nodded. "It's a Gerber Daisy."

He grinned. "That's cheating."

"I didn't study for this test."

He laughed. "Fair enough." He started toward the door. "Are you ready for your next test?"

She cringed slightly, then laughed. "I guess so. I think so." Stepping past him toward the door she admitted. "I'm not sure."

Laughing he replied, "Fair enough."

They climbed into the truck and he wracked his brain thinking where he could go next. Then he nodded, he knew.

He pulled into the lot in front of Lara's Delights.

She laughed. "You want to know if I want to eat cookies or bake them?"

"Either one is a revelation, isn't it?"

Laughing she said, "I suppose it is."

They strutted to the front door, hand in hand, the

mood lifted and his new mission was helping Everleigh figure out what she wanted to be when she grew up. He was up for the mission.

The aromas that wafted over them in Lara's place were mouthwatering.

"Oh, this is so cute in here."

Lara appeared from the kitchen in the back. "Hi, Henry." She walked forward and held her hand out to Everleigh. "I presume you're Everleigh. I'm Lara Vickers."

"Yes, I am. It's nice to meet you, Lara. Henry wants to know if I like eating cookies or baking them more."

Lara cocked her head to the side. "Okay."

He laughed. "We're trying to figure out what Everleigh would like to do in her spare time. To date, she's all work and no play."

Lara laughed. "Oh, okay. That makes a bit more sense." She hurried behind the counter and pulled out two cookies, decorated like flowers. She laid them each on a paper plate and handed them out to each of them. "These are on the house. Let me know if you like them."

Everleigh giggled. "I see a pattern here with the flowers."

He chuckled, "Completely unintended."

He put money on the counter and winked at Lara. "I appreciate the freebie, but I don't want you doing that. You have a baby to pay for soon enough."

Lara laughed. "I think we'll be fine with baby things. But thank you. I appreciate it."

Everleigh grinned. "Congratulations. When are you due?"

"February. I have a ways to go. Luckily for me, I haven't been sick in the mornings, so that's a bonus. I don't know how I'd bake cookies with morning sickness."

"That would be terrible."

Lara's phone rang. "Gotta get this. Henry, you two grab something to drink and take a seat wherever you like."

"Thanks, Lara."

He led Everleigh to a little table in front of the large front window. "What would you like to drink?"

The smile she shined on him nearly buckled his knees. "A water would be great."

He turned, swallowed the knot in his throat and pulled two bottles of water from the cooler near the counter.

Sitting across from Everleigh, he grinned at her and nodded to her cookie. "Eat up."

She lifted her cookie and took a bite out of it. She closed her eyes and sat back in her chair. "Mmm." Swallowing, she breathed. "That's to-die-for good."

"I believe I told you, best cookies you'll ever eat."

16

Everleigh grinned, then swallowed the delicious bite of cookie in her mouth. "You were right. Are right. You are right."

Sipping from her water bottle, she bit into her cookie once again. Henry watched her. His lips turned up at the corners and it was hard to look away from him. The man was positively enticing.

He nodded and bit into his cookie. His eyes stared into hers and she couldn't look away.

He swallowed the last bite of his cookie, washed it down with water then his lips spread open into a breath-taking smile. "Well?"

"Well, what?" She responded.

"Eating cookies or baking them?"

"Oh." She chuckled and took a drink of water. "Eating them. To be honest, I don't know how to cook. I guess I'd be a pathetic housemate or wife. I've lived most of my adult life on military bases or in hotel rooms. So, I eat what is available at the local grocery stores or when all else fails, I'll stop at a diner."

He stared at her a moment and she thought he'd be a great poker player, because she couldn't guess the direction of his thoughts.

"That's sad. Honey, you haven't had an actual life."

The heat crawled up her chest, it burned her cheeks and her ears. Her breathing caught in her throat. Words escaped her. A slight panic crawled through her body. He thought she was pathetic.

His right hand stretched across the table and wrapped her left hand in its warmth. His fingers squeezed gently. His voice was soft when he said, "Maybe to some I haven't had an actual life either. I grew up playing war games, served in the military, and now work for GHOST. You may well think my life has been weird. But I have friends I've known and trusted for my entire life. I feel like you've never had the opportunity to stay in one place long enough to make friends. Is that a fair assessment?"

A knot the size of a watermelon grew in her throat, and she swallowed several times to loosen it enough to eradicate it.

"That's fair." His fingers lifted her chin so her eyes looked into his. And they were stunning. Deep blue eyes surrounded by dark lashes. His dark hair and olive coloring made the blue look unearthly.

"I didn't say that to embarrass you. I'm trying to understand you. What your life has been and what you want it to be moving forward."

Her lips trembled into a soft smile. "Okay."

"We have to ask the hard questions to find out the truth. Isn't that what you told Simek today when he balked at your questions?"

She chuckled remembering her own words. His hand left her chin and she felt the loss. "Yes. Touché."

He chuckled slightly and finished the last of his water. She watched his throat move as he swallowed the cool liquid. Then she asked, "But why do you care?"

He twisted the plastic cap onto his empty water bottle and stared into her eyes. "I care. I want you to be happy. I sense you aren't." His right shoulder lifted and fell.

She finished her water and Henry stood. He gathered their plates and water bottles and tossed them in the wastebasket near the door. He called out, "See you later, Lara."

She poked her head out of the kitchen, "Bye, Henry. Nice to meet you, Everleigh."

Henry pulled his truck from the parking lot at Lara's and turned them toward her hotel. He seemed contemplative. She was perplexed. To say no one ever cared this much about her life, besides her, was an understatement. To know Henry cared was overwhelming. It was also exciting. He truly was the total package.

She turned to stare at his profile. It was strong and handsome. "But, WHY do you care?"

His head twisted and their eyes met. "I do the job I do because I care about others. I protect those who can't protect themselves. I cause pain, sometimes physical, sometimes legally, to those who hurt others. I care about people."

She swallowed and stared out the windshield. "Oh."

He pulled them into the parking lot of her hotel. She unfastened her seatbelt. "You don't have to walk me in. I'll see you in a little while?"

"Yes, ma'am. I'll be here at five forty-five."

"See you then."

She exited and as she reached the door of the hotel, she turned to see him watching her. Butterflies spun around in her tummy as she saw the intensity of his gaze. She smiled and waved and he waved in return. She stepped through the door of the hotel and a plethora of emotions assaulted her at once. Her stomach flipped and fluttered. Her eyes watered. Her knees - where had they gone? She worried if she took a step forward, she'd surely fall flat on her face. She stood stock-still for a moment. Silent counts to ten to settle herself before moving forward.

Finally feeling able to walk, she quietly moved through the lobby and to the elevator. She needed a nap, a shower, and a call to her sister. Likely in that order. What she didn't know is who Everleigh Hayes really was. She'd been told all her life who to be. But Henry made her question all of that. Did she want to learn to cook? She did. She wanted to know how to be self-sufficient. She wanted a home base. A place to call home. That way, when she was between jobs, she wouldn't have to live like a nomad or camp out at her sister's place. Not that she didn't like it, but she didn't want to have to go there because she had nowhere else to go.

Her heart raced at the realization. She wanted a home base. She did. Her fingers shook as she pulled her shoes off and neatly lined them up with the others on the floor of the closet. She removed her suit and hung it neatly in the closet. Her blouse needed to be laundered and she put it in the laundry bag, for the hotel to wash. She'd never done a load of laundry in her life. How did they do that? Her parents were both career military and only used a laundry service associated with the military wherever they lived. In so many ways, she was like a young child. So many things she needed to learn about actually living on her own. It was overwhelming.

She climbed between the sheets of her bed and fell asleep quickly.

17

H enry texted Everleigh. "I'm in the lobby."
Her text returned quickly. "I'm on my way
down."

He pocketed his phone, pushed his hands in his
trouser pockets and waited. His eyes darted toward the
elevator often, though he kept his eyes on his surround-
ings - force of habit. The soft chime of the elevator
reached his ears, and he quickly turned his head. An older
couple stepped out and his shoulders slumped slightly.

His eyes followed the older couple as they left the
building, his hand at the small of her back, as he escorted
her to their car. After she sat in the car, he closed the door
and grinned at her as he strutted around the front.

The elevator chimed again and he turned to see the
loveliest sight. Everleigh practically glided toward him,
wearing a white sun dress with sunflowers printed on it. It
swayed with her body. Her long blonde hair draped over
her shoulders, her feet were wrapped in heeled sandals.
The polish on her toenails was soft pink to match her
fingernails.

He swallowed to wet his throat. "You look beautiful."

Her smile was so bright it lit the room. She was radiant. "Thank you. You look very handsome."

He wanted to hug her. Pull her to his body and feel her against him. He settled for placing his hand at the small of her back as they moved in unison toward his truck.

She stepped gracefully, as always, into his truck, and he spent the trip around his truck breathing in and out deeply to get his emotions under control. He'd been on dates with beautiful women before. This wasn't his first rodeo, or his second. But he didn't remember feeling this way about any of them. Excited, nervous, anxious, all rolled into one.

Moving toward the exit of the hotel driveway, Everleigh chuckled. "I visited Shianne today and got this dress."

He grinned. "You selected well. It looks stunning on you. Or maybe you make the dress stunning. Either way, it's a great pairing."

Her cheeks brightened. "Thank you."

"What did you think of Shianne?"

Everleigh turned her head to face him. "She's...vibrant."

He burst out laughing. "That's a great way to describe her."

"So you know her."

"She's Lara's best friend. She's been to the HOG a fair amount. She also shopped for Elena and her mom when we brought them down off the mountain. She about drove us all from the room in her excitement."

"She told me about that. It was a big deal for her."

"I gathered."

Everleigh was quiet for a while. As he pulled into the

parking lot of Porter's, she softly said. "I've given our chat this afternoon a lot of thought."

His eyes slid to hers. "In what way?"

"In the way that I need to begin thinking about what I want for me. Who I want to be. What I want to do with my life." She smiled. "This is the start of it. I bought a pretty frilly dress instead of a business suit. I can't remember the last time I had a casual dress to just go out in. I own business suits and workout clothing."

He grinned at her and when she returned his grin, his heartbeat matched the rhythm of "Wipe Out" by Steppenwolf.

"I'm happy you're taking steps for yourself. Life is about more than work. It should be enjoyed and lived."

A truck pulled in alongside his, and his mom waved from the passenger seat. He waved in return, then said, "Are you ready?"

"Yes."

As he held her hand to help her from the truck, the electricity he felt at this small touch sizzled up his arm. He shivered slightly but couldn't process it because his mom came around the front of the truck. "I've heard all good things about Porter's."

"Did everyone at the HOG fill you in today?"

"They sure did." She hugged him briefly. "Everleigh, you are stunning." His mom leaned in and hugged Everleigh as he watched. They looked natural together. He filled his lungs with air and turned to his dad and hugged him. "How are you, Henry? We didn't see you much today."

"I'm good. I'm sorry I didn't have more time with you."

"We understand completely. Let's go catch up."

His dad held his arm out toward his mom, and she

gracefully swooped into his fold. They sauntered into Porter's casually chatting, his dad's hand on the small of his mom's back. He chuckled to himself.

He turned to Everleigh and held his hand out to her. Her lips turned up into a beautiful smile as she laid her hand in his. As they reached the door to Porter's, he opened the door, then ushered her in with his hand at the small of her back. He liked it there better.

"Do you have reservations?" The hostess asked.

Henry stepped forward. "Yes. Delany for four."

The hostess glanced at her book, then nodded. "Right this way, please."

She ushered them to the outdoor patio where he and Everleigh had eaten yesterday. As he held Everleigh's chair out for her, the hostess informed them, "We have a special guest tonight. Mr. Zachary Malloy is in town and he's agreed to come in and play for us. If you've never had the pleasure, he's amazing! He's a one-time local, but now he travels around singing for his supper."

His mom giggled. "That sounds lovely."

They were handed menus and as they looked the menus over, a man in a cowboy hat and new jeans sat behind a microphone and pulled a guitar over his shoulder.

"Good evening, ladies and gentlemen. My name is Zachary Malloy, and I'm honored to entertain you this evening."

He strummed his guitar and sang a song Henry had never heard before. The waitress came by and took their drink and food orders. They settled in to enjoy the evening when their drinks were delivered. Henry's mom held her glass up.

"I'd like to congratulate Henry on the purchase of his

new farm. Zander and I managed to email back and forth today, and Mr. DeWitt has signed your offer. Since you don't need to obtain financing, we've arranged for you to take possession on Friday. We'll still have paperwork to complete at a later date once the title company has managed their due diligence, and paperwork. But Mr. DeWitt has agreed that you'll rent it from him until final paperwork is completed in about three weeks. Rent is one dollar."

His heartbeat sped up and he momentarily lost the ability to speak. His dad raised his glass as did Everleigh. In unison they said, "Congratulations."

He tapped his glass to theirs. "Thank you all so much. Mom, seriously, thank you for managing all of that. It's incredible."

"I'd do anything for you Henry. And Stella of course."

Mr. Malloy started singing "Tennessee Whiskey" and his dad stood. He held his hand out to his mom, "Luna. Dance with me. I've loved this song since I first heard it. I've loved you since I first saw you. It's fitting."

Her smile radiated love. He watched them glide to the dance floor, which was nothing more than a small space cleared out in front of Mr. Malloy.

Everleigh smiled. "Why does he call her Luna?"

He stared at his parents as they moved together like two pieces of a puzzle. "My mom's grandfather called her Luna because her light-colored hair and her soft demeanor reminded him of the moon. My dad loved the story so much, he began calling her Luna immediately."

"Oh, that's so sweet."

He turned to Everleigh, "Would you like to dance?"

She laughed. "I'd love to."

He stood and held his hand out to hers. They glided to

the floor and the instant he turned and pulled her into his arms, it was as if fireworks went off in his head, and his body. He struggled for clear thoughts for a few moments, so he pulled her in tightly and swayed with her to the song. He'd never hear this song again without thinking of Everleigh Hayes.

18

Her stomach was a jumbled mess. Her fingers shook and so did her knees. She had an incredible attraction to Henry Delany. This man, he was turning her head. She no longer thought only of her next job, but of him. She went shopping to buy an outfit for him. Well, it was for her, but to impress him. Now, here she was on the dance floor with him, his beefy arms wrapped around her body and pulling her in close and she was grateful to just be here. She didn't try to talk to him because she honestly couldn't form words right now. If she had to think of something to say, something stupid would pop out of her mouth for certain. How incredibly embarrassing that would be. She was a top-notch negotiator, she couldn't ever be heard saying something stupid. She'd never get another job.

Henry's head dipped down. His lips were near her ear, and when he whispered, had he not been holding her, she certainly would have melted in a puddle.

"I've thought about holding you like this all day. How

fortunate there's music here tonight to make it easier for me to do so."

She swallowed the enormous lump in her throat. "You have no idea how many times I've thought about being in your arms." Kinda stupid. Sappy. Reputation ruining. Not really. It was the honest-to-goodness truth.

She heard his ragged breathing. She heard him whisper, "Jesus." She felt him harden against her lower belly and it took monumental strength not to push herself tighter to him. She'd never in her life hear this song again and not think of Henry Delany.

Sadly, the song ended and she'd now have to walk with rubbery knees to the table. She inhaled a deep breath and stepped back slightly. She tilted her head to see Henry looking down at her with the sexiest smile she'd ever seen. S-E-X-Y.

Henry's mom, Roxanne, approached. "Isn't that the sexist song? We both love it so much."

"It is. Mr. Malloy sings it very well." She managed to say.

Henry walked beside her to the table, his hand holding hers. His aftershave had seeped into her pores as they danced, and she hoped her new dress absorbed as much as it could so she could smell him in her room all night.

Just as they sat, Tate and Lara stopped at their table. "Hi, everyone. All the talk about Porter's at the house got us hungry, so Lara and I decided to have dinner out tonight."

Hawk laughed. "Join us. Please."

Lara chuckled. "We don't want to interrupt."

Lara's eyes darted to hers. She smiled brightly, "It's not an interruption. Please join us."

She scooted her chair over and Henry followed. Tate sat next to Henry and Lara sat across from him. She was quietly grateful for more people at the table to fill in any awkward silences. Not that there had been any. But this felt like a 'meeting the parents' kind of dinner, even though it wasn't an official date. At least not on Henry's part. On hers, it was the first date she'd been on in years. And she liked Henry. Really, liked him. So, in her mind, this was a date.

She should probably not accept any more offers of dinner from Henry. She could feel herself growing attached. She'd be leaving, likely in a week or so, it would only make it harder for her to go.

Lara said, "Everleigh, how do you feel negotiations are going?"

She smiled. "Tomorrow will be a tell. So far, I've only met with one side of the issue. Tomorrow, I meet with Craig and his council."

Tate shook his head. "You should make Craig come down here."

"It won't do any good to put him on further defense by starting out with forcing him to come down to what he considers enemy territory."

Tate shrugged. "He's going to need to learn we're not the enemy down here. At least most of us aren't. More people than not want this nonsense to be over and the sooner he learns that he can come down here and talk to us, the sooner we find a path to peace."

"That may be, but forcing the issue won't start that process. It'll inflame it before it starts."

Roxanne spoke up. "Everleigh's right. Let Craig think her coming to him is a first step. The next conversation with Craig will need to be down here."

Everleigh nodded. "Yes. Thank you."

Henry leaned back and put his arm across the back of her chair. His thumb brushed her shoulder, soothingly. Back and forth. She sat perfectly still as the conversation switched to baby talk and whether or not Tate and Lara had settled on any names. She was happy to sit back and feel Henry's connection to her, though it was hidden from all the others. She could feel his warmth across her shoulders. His thumb brushing slowly against her left shoulder. She'd sit like this as long as he wanted her too.

Hawk looked at her then, a soft smile on his face. "Everleigh, when do you have to leave for your next job?"

There it was. The buzzkill moment. Henry's thumb stilled and she felt his arm stiffen behind her shoulders. "As soon as I'm finished here Casper has another job for me in North Carolina, I believe. He's still confirming." She said sadly.

Roxanne's eyes darted to Henry. Everleigh didn't look at him. Lara stiffened slightly and, thank god the waitress came with their food.

Henry removed his arm from behind her and the sadness that filled her stomach nearly made her cry. The waitress set her plate before her and the smell of the food didn't smell nearly as enticing as it had last night. Roxanne started the conversation again. "Oh, this smells so good."

Hawk agreed and so did Tate.

She straightened her shoulders, picked up her fork and knife and sliced off a small piece of steak. It was a bad idea for her to come tonight.

19

Henry pulled into the parking lot of the Homeland Guest House and parked at the outer edge of the lot. He backed in so they could see the parking lot and front of the building, but he wanted a few moments alone with Everleigh.

"Do you really have to leave after this is over?" His voice sounded hoarse, even to him.

"Casper called me today and said he had something lined up. I'm to let him know when I believe I'll be wrapping up here."

"Do you want to?"

She turned her head to look at him. He met her gaze. "Go?"

"Yes."

She bit her bottom lip and that was enticing as fuck. She was enticing as fuck.

She inhaled deeply. It was impossible not to watch her chest rise and fall. "I don't think so."

He swallowed. There was that. "Then why do it?"

"What else am I supposed to do? I can't only eat cookies for a living."

"What living expenses do you have?"

He saw her eyes well with tears. "Thank you for pointing out what a loser I am. I have nothing. Are you happy? I am nothing but a workhorse for others. I've only just begun to start thinking about me. Until I know what else is available to me, I don't have anything."

A shiny silvery tear slid down her cheek and he reached out and swiped it away with the back of his forefinger. "I'm sorry. I absolutely did not mean to make you cry. I also don't think you're a loser. Just the opposite. But how will you have the time to figure out what you want to do when you're running from job to job?"

She sniffed daintily. He almost chuckled it was so cute. She huffed out a breath. "I don't know."

He reached over and laid his hand on her shoulder. "Hey. Look at me."

Her head slowly turned, her glistening eyes looked surreal in the darkness of the night, with the outside lights capturing the moisture. "You must have a ton of vacation time built up. Take a few weeks. Stay here. You can stay with me. We'll see what we learn about who Everleigh Hayes is."

She swallowed. "That'll just make it harder to leave."

"Because you like me?"

"Yes." It was a whisper.

"I like you too. I mean so much more than like you. I like Lara. I really like you."

She chuckled. "I really like you too." She swiped at her eyes. "That sounded rather grade school."

They both chuckled. He finally added, "I suppose it

did. But my feelings are more than any grade-school boy has ever had for a girl."

He leaned over the console, slowly, his left hand held the side of her head and his lips touched hers. Softly, ever so softly. He brushed little kisses on her lips. They felt good together. Her lips against his was like a balm. He kissed her longer. Holding his lips to hers. Softly. His tongue slowly swiped across her lips and hers parted. He slid his tongue along hers, swirling and tasting her. The wine she had at dinner mixed with her perfume was like a drug. His head tilted to the side and their lips fit together perfectly as their tongues danced a slow, smooth rhythm. "Tennessee Whisky." Sultry. Heavenly.

He reluctantly pulled back and stared into her eyes. "That was fantastic."

"Yeah. Wow." She whispered.

He grinned. "I've thought about doing that a lot."

Her lips turned up in a breathtaking smile. "Me too."

Headlights swooped around the truck and he turned to watch an older truck slowly cruise the parking lot. It didn't appear to be looking for a parking spot, there were several to choose from. Slowly, it pulled into the spot next to Everleigh's SUV. Her brows furrowed as the truck parked.

Two men got out of the truck and walked around Everleigh's SUV. Her hand reached for the door handle, and he reached his arm out and grabbed her left hand. "Don't."

"But that's my car."

"I know. But you can't approach them. They have weapons."

"How do you know?"

"I saw a sidearm on the driver."

He picked up his phone and tapped Tate's number.

"Hey, there."

"Tate. I'm at the hotel and two men in an older pickup just parked next to Everleigh's SUV and got out."

A loud pop sounded.

"And, I believe they just popped her tire. Run these plates." He craned his neck to see the plates clearly. "TCB389".

"Hang tight. Are you and Everleigh safe?"

"For now, we haven't been spotted."

Another loud pop sounded and she gasped. He held her hand tighter and turned to face her. He shook his head. "It'll be alright."

"But, they're..."

"I know."

"Those plates are stolen." Tate replied.

"BRR?"

"That would be my guess."

"So Craig decided to send a message before tomorrow's negotiation meeting."

"It appears so. If you don't think she'll be safe there, bring her to the HOG. We have plenty of room."

"I'll talk to her and see what she wants to do."

"Keep me posted."

The call ended and he turned to Everleigh. "We think it's the BRR. I'm sure you heard all of that. They know you're here. You're welcome to come to the HOG. It's safe there. We have security and room."

"I've never had anything like this happen before. Negotiations have gotten tense, but never a personal attack on me."

"It's not necessarily a personal attack. You're just the face and name to bringing them down the mountain and working to pay taxes. It's a stall tactic. A bad one, but one nonetheless."

The two men got in the truck and sped out of the parking lot. Henry leaned toward the windshield and stared at the driver. "No shit! That's Craig driving."

Everleigh swallowed and he continued to hold her hand. "Do you want to go back to the HOG with me?"

She shook her head slowly. "I want you to stay here with me."

He stared into her eyes for a long time. His mind told him she was leaving soon. His body told him to run to the door as fast as he could. His heart told him it would break when she left.

His body won.

20

E verleigh glanced at her SUV as Henry hurried her along to the door. "Why can't we go look at it?"

"I don't know if they're watching. We'll call the sheriff from inside. They'll leave as soon as they see the squad coming."

"Okay." Her brows bunched together so tightly she felt it. "But what does it matter if they see us?"

"They may ambush us. My job is to protect you, Everleigh. Not your vehicle."

He ushered her into the building, and she tried not turning back to look at her car. It was honestly the only thing she owned. Besides her clothes. But her car was like her home. Sort of. She didn't sleep in it, but she had a bit of an attachment to it. Likely an unhealthy attachment because it was all she had.

She sucked in a lungful of air. She was thirty years old and all she had to show for her life was a vehicle. She had a lot of money in the bank. There was that at least.

They stepped into the elevator, and she pushed the button to the second floor. She inhaled and exhaled to settle her nerves. She'd never been attacked before. Not that she had been attacked bodily, but it sure felt personal.

She glanced up at Henry. "Do you think they'd come inside here?"

Henry's shoulders rose and fell. "He's never been that bold. Then again, he's never had his back against the wall like this. This will finalize the end of the BRR. Already some of his people have jobs down here and are trying to blend in. Once the treaty is amended and they are forced to pay back property taxes, and the children will have to come down to school, his power is diminished. He's never known any life but the one he's now losing."

The elevator door opened, and she stepped out and moved toward her room. Her fingers shook as she pulled her little metal key from her little handbag. This hotel still used metal keys, it was quaint. Henry reached down and plucked the key from her hand. He lifted her hand and kissed her fingers. "I'll protect you."

She swallowed the lump that sat in her throat. He'd protect her. When had anyone ever said that to her? The answer was never. Never in her life did another human being tell her they'd protect her.

Her lips quivered. "Thank you."

He opened her door, pushed it open and waited for her to walk in. She noticed him glance both ways down the hall to make sure no one was around. Inside, he closed the door, and twisted the locks, then stalked to the window and peered through a crack in the curtains to see what was outside. Or maybe who was outside.

She put her hand over her tummy as she realized, she'd invited Henry to spend the night with her. He probably thought they'd have sex. She hadn't meant it totally, initially. But she kind of did. If they had sex, it would be dangerous to her heart. It would break her heart when she left here. Because...Henry. She'd know him biblically, as they said. He'd know her the same way. It was a dangerous game she was playing. She'd never been a thrill seeker. But he brought something out in her. Something that made her not want to be lonely anymore. She didn't want to be alone. She wanted to feel Henry touch her. To feel him kiss her again. To...feel.

She set her handbag on the desk and sat to unbuckle her sandals. He turned and the look he landed on her took her breath away. His nostrils flared and his eyes blazed a trail to her hand unbuckling her sandal. His eyes then sizzled her skin as they roamed up her leg. It. Was. Exhilarating.

He pulled his phone from his pocket and tapped a couple of times. She stared at his fingers. His hands. His arms. He exuded sensuality. Even his fingers were muscular. Thick, strong fingers that deftly tapped on the phone, which looked impossibly small in his beefy hand.

He pulled the phone to his ear, his eyes, those beautiful dark blue eyes, stared at her. Her eyes locked together with his. Her heartbeat increased and her breathing stuttered.

"This is Henry Delany. I'm located at the Homeland Guest House. Everleigh Hayes, who is a guest here, and I witnessed Craig Howard and a comrade, slash the tires of Everleigh Hayes's vehicle."

His jaw tightened. His breathing seemed rapid and shallow as if this had happened to him. She swallowed to moisten her throat and stood, taking her sandals with her to the closet in her room. Gently laying her sandals neatly inside, she stared at her business suits and her shoulders slumped.

Moving to the old wooden dresser along the wall across from her closet, she opened the top drawer and stared dismally at her underwear. She'd purposely kept her clothing to a minimum so she didn't have so much to pack.

Pulling a pair of pajamas from the drawer, she turned toward the bathroom, then stopped. What if they had to run out at a moment's notice? Maybe she should put on some workout clothing and tennis shoes. She could run fast in those. Of course they'd hardly be running. Henry's truck was here. The police were coming. There would be all kinds of people here soon. She dug through the drawer once again, then stepped into the bathroom with a gray and fuchsia workout outfit she'd had laundered this morning. It was cute. She liked it, which meant she felt good in it.

A glance at Henry showed him watching her intently. Those eyes. My god, those eyes. They made her stupid. Thoughts left her head. What a silly thing to have happen to a woman in her thirties.

Stepping into the bathroom, she silently closed the door. Resting her back against it, she swallowed again, then practiced even breathing. She was way over her head here. She wasn't even sure he was interested in her. At least for more than a tumble in the sheets or two.

But honestly, that wouldn't be bad, would it? It had been years. She liked him. Lord, he was sexy, and smart, and oh so yummy. Yes, it wouldn't be a bad thing.

21

Henry sat on the foot of the bed. He scraped his hand through his hair then closed his eyes. Rotating his shoulders, he stretched then glanced out the window once more. The faint blue hue down the road told him someone from the sheriff's office was coming. Craig had gotten very bold. But who wouldn't, when their life seemed to be out of control and about to slip away.

He paced in the small space, reminding himself not to think of Everleigh in the bathroom, likely naked, and looking fine. It only made him stupid to think of her that way. He couldn't afford to be stupid right now. Not ever, but certainly not now. Not with Everleigh's life in the balance.

The bathroom door opened and he sucked in a breath when she exited wearing gray spandex workout shorts and a matching top. Her body was enticing. Slender and tall, she had curves in all the right places, and his eyes were glued on those places.

"The sheriff is on his way." His voice was soft. He had

to force sound to come out. Clearing his throat, he tried again. "They'll be here in a second."

"Okay. Should I change clothes?"

All too quickly, he said, "No." He shook his head slightly, "I'll go down and see if they'll allow us to come in tomorrow to make a statement."

"Okay." Her hand was pressed against her tummy and he felt sorry for her. This wasn't her line of work.

"It'll be fine. If you'll feel better, you can come back with me to the HOG and you can stay there. You'll be safe and we have the rooms."

"I don't think it's bad enough for that yet. Do you?"

"I only want you to feel safe. If staying somewhere else is what you want, I have the place for you. Otherwise, I'll be here with you and we'll deal with whatever we have to deal with together, here."

"Thank you." She moved toward him as though there was a magnetic pull. He felt it. She reached forward and wrapped her arms around his waist. He bent down slightly and kissed the top of her head. She felt good against him. His arms wrapped her tightly, and his body shielded her from the world. At least that's what he wanted to do.

After a few moments, she stepped back, her head tilted up to him and her eyes looked into his. The green in her eyes reminded him of the grass on his farm. Her lashes created the dark fan around them, and her full lips parted slightly.

He dipped his head and kissed her lips. Softly, but fully. They parted further and he slid his tongue inside her mouth. She was warm and compliant. Her tongue danced with his. Their lips fit together like pieces of a puzzle. His hands roamed down her back and cupped her ass. She moaned and the vibration against his lips sent his body into a spin. He deepened their kiss, his hands touching her where he could. His hands lifted slightly and slid inside the back of her clingy spandex shorts, her soft skin underneath revved his engines. She moaned again and his excitement inched up a notch. Her hands slid down to his ass and squeezed and his breathing stuttered.

She slipped her hands between the waistband on his jeans and his boxer briefs, though the tightness didn't allow her to move down. Which was fucking annoying. Fucking. Annoying.

His phone rang and he harrumphed out a breath. Laying his forehead against hers, he sucked in some air and muttered, "Fuck."

"Yes." She whispered. He got the distinct impression she thought he was asking.

Swallowing, he pulled back only enough to take his phone from his pocket. "Delany."

Everleigh slowly slid her fingers around his waistband to the front of his jeans, her fingers doing maddening things to his brain. She was absolutely making him stupid. Stupid!

"I'm sorry. Who is this?"

"Sheriff Cranford."

"I'm sorry, Sheriff. Your voice was muffled."

He watched Everleigh's lips part slightly, the corners of her mouth turning up into a coy, sexy smile. She unbuttoned his jeans, licked her lips, which sent his brain right out the window. Then she lowered the zipper on his jeans.

"Sorry. I had it under my chin. We're out here. Yes, her tires are slashed. You can come down and make a statement now or tomorrow."

"Tomorrow." His voice was husky. So husky he even recognized it didn't sound like him.

"Tomorrow will be fine. We'll be out here for a while. Then, we'll pack it up. One of my deputies is following Craig. He was sitting across the road in Shianne's parking lot watching."

"Thank you. I suspected he was watching."

"Okay. Enjoy your evening."

He. Had. No. Idea.

Dropping his phone to the desk, he slid his hands under Everleigh's arms and pulled her up his body. Her legs immediately wrapped around his waist and he bored into her eyes. "This could get messy."

"Yes." She kissed his lips lightly then pulled back.

"My duty comes first."

She planted light feathery kisses on his jaw and to his ear. "Okay."

"Fuck." He grumbled.

"Yes."

He stepped to the bed. His knee hit first, and he lifted her toward the middle of the bed. Laying her down, and falling with her, he held himself over her with his elbows. His lips kissed her lips, this time with enough pressure to let her know he was absolutely serious. She kissed him back with the same intensity.

Before he could register another coherent thought, they were arms and legs moving, touching, lips tasting, fingers exploring. He managed to pull her workout shorts off and found the softness between her legs with his fingers. She gasped as his fingers slid into her body. Her legs opened to give him better access and he slipped his fingers in and out enjoying the feel and sound their bodies made.

Her fingers tugged at his jeans, and his shirt and finally he'd managed to remove all of his clothing. He stood and bent to snag his jeans off the floor, grabbing a condom from his wallet. Instead of climbing back up the bed, he bent over her and licked the seam of her pussy. The gasp she made caused his lips to curl up into a smile. He suckled and licked her as her fingers dug into his hair and finally pulled his head up to hers.

"Inside me. Please."

He chuckled slightly. Slipping the condom onto his penis, he hovered over her, staring into her eyes as he slid himself slowly inside of her. Once he'd seated himself fully, his eyes closed and he halted just a moment to feel her. She felt warm, and tight and so fucking amazing, he shivered.

Opening his eyes, he saw her watching him. Her eyes darted back and forth, watching every move on his face.

"You are without a doubt the sexiest man I've ever known."

He moved out and back in and her breathing stuttered.

"You are the sexiest woman I've ever met, Everleigh Hayes."

He moved in her, in and out. She moved with him. The world's oldest dance and they were excellent dance partners. Move for move they danced with perfection. Changing their rhythm when they needed, each following the other until her eyes rounded and her body jerked as her orgasm flew through her. He pumped twice more and his orgasm spiraled through his body and left him weak once he'd finished. He held himself above her, their breathing ragged, their bodies limp. Once he could move he rolled over and she rolled with him, so her body lay half on his, her arm and leg tossed over his body in an effort to keep him close. He loved it. It felt right.

22

She woke first. Her arms and legs tangled with Henry's. She lay there, remembering their night, enjoying waking to him in her bed. His presence was everything. She felt safe with him beside her. She felt loved the way he made love to her. She felt fulfilled in their joining. All feelings she'd never known before.

His arm tightened around her shoulders and squeezed. "Did you sleep good?"

"Yes. You?"

"Yes. Better than I have in a very long time."

"Me too."

"Hmm. That's something, isn't it?"

She giggled. "I'd say it is."

She lifted herself up and glanced at the clock. "I have to get into the shower. Do you know if Craig is coming down here or if I have to go up there?"

"I'll call the mayor. I'm guessing the fact the sheriff was chasing him last night will mean he'll stubbornly stay up there."

"Right." She slid off the side of the bed and rummaged

through her drawers for undergarments. Moving to the closet she pulled out a gray suit. Then, chancing a glance at Henry, saw him watching her.

"You're a gorgeous woman, Everleigh."

She blew him a kiss and ducked into the bathroom to shower.

Once she felt fresh and presentable, she opened the bathroom door and stepped out to a cup of coffee.

Henry grinned. "I thought you might like some coffee. I need at least three cups in the morning."

"Thank you."

Sipping her coffee, she glanced at her phone and saw an email from the mayor. Tapping it, she read his message.

"Craig is refusing to come down here. You'll need to go up. Henry will be with you and Myles from GHOST will be joining you."

Looking up at Henry, who was dressed only in boxer briefs and was incredibly yummy, she said, "Did you see the message from the mayor?"

"Yes."

His shoulders were stiff, his posture rigid. His muscles twitched. It was hard to look away. "You don't like it."

"It's his turf. He knows that ground like the back of his hand. I had hoped he'd be willing to negotiate, and his first concession would be coming down here. After last night, I don't like going up there at all."

Her heartbeat sped as she watched Henry's body change from the sexy, accommodating man last night to this special operative who had a mission to perform.

He stood and pulled the curtains back, his eyes exploring the entire parking lot. When he turned back to her, he inhaled deeply as he stepped closer. He pulled her into a hug, and she needed that. Really needed it. Her arms circled his body, his warm skin was a balm against hers. She pulled him as close as she could. His arms wrapped her tightly, his strength evident and needed.

"I won't let anything happen to you. For right now, I'm jumping in the shower. Don't go near the window, don't open the door for anyone."

"Okay."

"Promise."

"I promise."

He kissed the top of her head and disappeared into the bathroom, but he left the door open. She listened to him shower and imagined running soapy hands over every muscle. Big mistake. She needed her head straight. Today was the big day in negotiations.

Henry stepped from the bathroom, a white towel over his right shoulder, the end of the towel rubbing his hair dry.

She inhaled. "Do you think I should ignore what he did last night or let him know, we know, and address it?"

Henry moved and sat at the foot of the bed next to her. He turned slightly so he faced her and took her right hand in his. "I say, we go up and see what the mood is today. He's unpredictable. And, by unpredictable, I mean, unpredictable. You never know from one minute to the next when he'll explode. So, let's go up and sit down. Myles and I will be there. The sheriff will be close as well. My GHOST teammates will also be around, hidden in the shadows. There isn't one of them who wouldn't love a shot at Craig. So, it's no skin off anyone's nose to get into it with Craig. I'd bet my left nut, they're hoping they can take a shot at him."

She stared into his beautiful eyes and smiled. "I'd hate for you to give up a nut."

His laugh started deep in his chest and bubbled up through his throat. It was deep, and throaty, and incredibly sexy. She couldn't help smiling as she listened to his laughter. He dropped onto his back on the bed and pulled her down on top of him. His hands cupped her face and held her close as he kissed her lips. She felt him grow rigid as she slowly, catlike slow, moved over his body and straddled him. They let their lips mingle and move and test and taste. She loved every minute of it.

She wore a pencil skirt which slid up her hips, and now bunched around her lower abdomen. His hands roamed down her back to her ass and squeezed her cheeks, then pushed her onto his rigid length. She lightly gasped as he pushed and pulled her and hit. That. Spot.

With a finger, he slid her panties to the side, lowered his boxer briefs, and slid inside of her with ease. She moaned. He felt fantastic. His length filled her completely. His body moved with hers in such a way it was as if they were made for each other. They were intuitive with each other. It was dizzying, and fantastic. And she wanted more.

She laid her hands on his shoulders, feeling the muscles beneath and reveled in feeling them bunch and move. For her. All for her.

His hands helped her ride him. Up and down as their pace increased she felt her orgasm blaze through her body like a raging inferno. She cried out his name and his response was to push into her body harder until his orgasm slammed through him. She watched his face as it did and it was a site to behold. She'd never watched a man in pleasure. This man, she'd watch him forever. He was beautiful.

23

Henry drove with a new determination to do his job to the best of his ability. He'd protect Everleigh with his very life.

Everleigh sat stiffly in the seat next to him. Her hands laid upon the notebook she carried and her laptop case underneath. Both of them were steeling themselves for what was to come. Both of them hoped it would be a surprise-free day.

His eyes darted to the mirror and Myles's truck behind them. Maya, Spencer, and Adelaide were already in place somewhere on the mountain. Tate was at headquarters, or the HOG, manning communications and at the ready should the sheriff be called. The sheriff had squads parked at the bottom of the hill so as not to irritate Craig by coming onto 'his' land. But they were ready if they were needed. Truth be told, his team would eradicate Craig long before the sheriff or his deputies could get half-way up the hill. They'd said so when they met earlier this morning.

He turned a corner and where normally there'd be

guards on the road, none were visible. He had a communication unit in his ear and tapped it.

"No guards on the road."

"Copy." Myles replied. A few seconds later, Spencer, Maya, and Addy replied similarly.

He moved past the point where guards usually stood, his eyes peeled for any movement coming from the woods. Nothing. That set his nerves on high alert.

Tapping his comm unit to mute sound he said, "Remember, we aren't together. I'm your bodyguard. You're doing a job. I don't want him getting wind that you can be used for leverage."

"I got it."

He nodded slightly and tightened his hold on the steering wheel. Rounding another corner, he saw the first little cabin of many. He wasn't sure who lived in that one, they were dotted here and there up here. Anywhere there was a flat spot. The road became rockier, the truck bounced and rocked as he moved over the terrain.

Addy commented on the comm units, "Craig just walked out to their community gathering place or whatever they call it. He's sitting at a table to one end of the space. Right now, he's alone."

Tapping his unit, he replied. "Roger."

He stopped at a point the road no longer allowed passage and turned to Everleigh. "We'll have to walk from here. Stay close to me. Within reaching distance."

"Okay."

"I'll protect you."

She smiled but looked at her lap. "I know you will."

He opened his door and stepped down to the ground, then hurried around and opened Everleigh's door. He held his hand out to her and she waved him away. "I thought we weren't supposed to act like we're together."

"I can still use my manners." He hissed.

She complied and he squeezed her fingers slightly then let them go as they moved slowly toward Craig.

A group of kids, around eight, nine, or ten years old were working in a circle. It looked like they were processing vegetables. Peeling potatoes and chopping carrots.

Another group of younger children were being taught how to wash clothes. Everleigh's intake of breath caused him to turn to her. "Don't react."

"But they should be in school. Not laboring away."

"Don't react." His voice was especially stern.

Craig refused to look at them as they approached which he thought was incredibly rude. But Craig was Craig and there was no dealing with him and his bad behavior. Hopefully this would be over soon.

He approached Craig. "Craig Howard, this is Everleigh Hayes, the negotiator."

Craig turned his head. The up and down look he gave Everleigh made him want to pluck his eyes out. Slowly. Painfully.

Everleigh held her hand out to shake, but Craig refused to shake it. Everleigh sat across the table from him, folded her hands on her notebook and waited.

They sat in silence for what felt like a long time and finally, Gerard Weston and his son, Jasiah, entered the meeting area. They were more cordial. Gerard held his hand out to Everleigh and shook it. Jasiah did the same. They introduced themselves and Gerard asked Everleigh if she'd like tea. She smiled and said she'd love some.

The smirk Craig made gave Henry the impression he

wanted her to have tea, which in turn caused Henry to intercept the tea and leave it on an empty table behind her. Myles carried a small pack and opened it up and pulled a cold water bottle out for Everleigh. She smiled then nodded.

Opening her laptop, and notebook, she started asking questions.

"Mr. Howard. I've recently met with the sheriff, the mayor, and the town council to get their ideas of what they'd like out of these negotiations. I'm here today to ask what you'd like from them."

Craig slowly turned his head and stared directly into her eyes. To Everleigh's credit, she didn't flinch, which made him so fucking proud of her. "I want the whole lot to go away and leave us alone. I don't want to pay taxes. I don't want my people to blend with theirs. I don't want our kids going to school. We're fine the way we are."

Everleigh wrote on her notebook, then typed in her laptop. She glanced at Gerard, "Mr. Weston, what do you want from these negotiations?"

Gerard folded his hands together and looked into Everleigh's eyes. "I'd like us to have a fair and equitable dividing of our responsibilities and theirs. We understand there are taxes due and some of our members have already found jobs in town. We'll start paying, but not until some utilities are brought up the mountain. If we pay our taxes, there's no enticement for the town to actually bring the utilities up here and we've lost our leverage."

Everleigh continued to type. "We'd like water brought up first. Then, electricity. In the future, we'd like the ability to have our own medical clinic up here so our people don't have to travel down so far, and our babies can be born up here. And, we have some talented people up here. Construction, carvers, bakers, artists, and more. We'd like them to be able to open their businesses up here if they want and not have to travel down to town. In the winter, the roads are treacherous, and it would be nice if the women didn't have to make the trip."

Everleigh smiled, "Isn't that possible now?"

"Who will come up here?"

"We can't force the townspeople to come up here. From what I'm told the biggest deterrent to them coming up here is the feeling they aren't safe. Only you can change that."

Gerard looked at Craig, the scowl on his face visible from a mile away. "Yes. I completely understand that."

"Have any of your people been harmed in town?" Everleigh asked.

Jasiah shook his head. "No. Actually right now we have five men working on a farm and they've said, while it was a bit rough in the beginning, they get along with everyone and the farmer is respectful and nice. We have Kent working in a computer shop and he likes it. A couple of the women have found cleaning jobs and they seem happy. And a couple of our women are working at the flower shop in town and they are happy."

Craig turned toward Jasiah. "How do you fucking know a damned thing?"

"Because I personally spoke to them to find out."

24

Everleigh's fingers shook as she typed. Craig's stare was enough to set her nerves on edge, but she refused to let him see it. Henry stood right behind her. Myles was near as well, watching the area to make sure they weren't ambushed. After what felt like hours and was actually, well, three hours, they'd gotten through all she needed to prepare her report and the next phase of this negotiation, which was the finalities. She looked at Gerard as she explained, ignoring Craig, since he was being an asshole.

"The next step will be for everyone to get together and work this out. The town hall is large enough and we've set the date for tomorrow morning at eight o'clock."

Craig bellowed. "I'm busy."

Everleigh turned to him and snipped. "Doing what, slashing someone's tires?"

The smirk on his face was about all she could tolerate.

Gerard's brows furrowed. "What's that all about?"

"Last night, Craig and an accomplice, came to the

hotel where I'm staying and slashed the tires on my vehicle."

Gerard turned to Craig. "You're so close to removal I can't believe you can't feel it."

"You don't have the fucking balls."

Jasiah leaned in to look past his father. "He does and so do I. All this talk about people needing to feel safe and you're doing everything you can to fuck this up."

"You don't know anything, boy."

"Jasiah. My name is Jasiah and I'm not your boy."

Craig stood and glared at Jasiah, which caused both Jasiah and Gerard to stand.

Henry leaned down and put his hand on her arm. "Stand up and get out of the way, Everleigh."

She stood and lifted her leg over the bench she sat on. Henry pulled her slightly behind him, his hands were at his sides and balled into tight fists.

Two men ran toward them, each taking a position between Gerard and Craig.

One of the men yelled, "That's enough. All of you stop it right now."

Gerard and Jasiah stood back. Gerard held his hands in the air in compliance.

She moved in front of Henry, though she stayed close. Addressing Gerard and Jasiah again, she said, "If Mr. Howard refuses to come down, the two of you will need to come down with the authority to make the agreement, if one is made."

Gerard nodded and held his hand out to shake. "We'll be there. If he isn't, we'll have the authority to enter into an agreement."

"Thank you." She turned and began moving to the

truck. She moved deliberately so she didn't show fear, but she wanted to get out of there - and now. She saw the children working again and froze.

Henry whispered in her ear, "Keep going."

"I can't."

She turned and addressed Gerard. "These children should be in school, not working like chattel."

Craig began racing toward her, "You don't fucking get to tell us how to raise our..."

A sharp thwack sounded as Henry's fist hit the left side of Craig's jaw. Craig went down like a two-thousand-pound rock, and she stared as he held his jaw in his hands and whimpered.

Gerard and Jasiah joined the group as they stared down at Craig. Gerard then looked into her eyes. "We agree with you and would like them to attend school. Please put that on your topics for tomorrow. Also, it looks as though Craig may not be able to speak much tomorrow, so God's watching over us."

Gerard nodded but said nothing else and Henry turned her around by the shoulders and ushered her to the truck.

He opened the door for her and used his left hand to help her in. She bit her bottom lip, knowing it was her fault his right hand likely hurt right now. He hustled around the truck and Myles did the same to his truck. The instant Henry had situated himself inside, he pushed the button to start his truck and she saw his hand had some swelling.

"I'm sorry."

He turned his truck around in a small clearing, then turned to look into her eyes. "Don't be. It was my pleasure.

That fucker has deserved that and more for a long fucking time."

She grinned and after a few beats he did as well.

Their descent down the mountain and to town gave her a few moments to ponder their conversation today and all that she'd witnessed. Craig would have to be removed. He refused and actually fought against any progress and he'd never ensure people were safe. Including his own. If they were going to fully integrate, he'd have to go. At least from a position of leadership. Which was really a dictatorship. She wished right now that she'd asked how many of their members were supporters of Craig.

"You did good today. I'm proud of you." Henry's voice was gruff and raspy, and goosebumps rose on her arms and legs. Her nipples pebbled tightly, and she inhaled a few deep breaths to keep her breathing even.

"Thank you. You have a wicked right cross."

He laughed and she stared at him. He was simply a beautiful man. Everything about him was all the stuff she loved in a man. Tall, strong, handsome. Ardent, ohh, the way he made her feel when they had sex was the stuff of dreams. He was perfect. At least for her.

He stopped laughing and turned onto the main road in Glen Hollow. She turned toward him and grinned. "We're going to your farm?"

"Not yet."

"I want to show you something."

He navigated the truck toward the back side of the mountain, down a country road and onto an old farm. Not his farm, but another one.

"The farmer gave me permission to drive through his field."

The field was bumpy, and she held onto the armrest tightly as they bounced across the ruts made by years of plowing and rain.

She clenched her teeth together so she didn't bite her tongue, until he finally came to a stop. He pointed up the mountain.

"This is the back side of Hickory Hills. There's less rock on this side. The town would need to bring the water out here to the farm and then likely a water tower large enough to handle the mountain. But it would be less expensive to go this route. We've never mentioned this to anyone on the town council. But last year when we snuck Elena and her mom down the mountain, we did it from this direction. There is some rock, but less than on the other side. It's in the extended plans for the town to bring water out here for the farmers anyway. The town wants to do it for the revenue, of course. It solves a few problems and work could feasibly begin right away."

"That's brilliant." She craned her neck to see what he pointed at, then turned to see the farm.

Henry continued explaining. "So, over to the left here, at the edge of this farmer's field, his name is Geoffrey Kurtz. He's now in his fifties and only keeps beef cows." He grinned. "So, at the edge of the field the town would need to purchase the land from Mr. Kurtz to build a water tower. I've spoken with him about the possibility and while he isn't excited to start paying for his water, he's willing to do it to keep the peace. I thought maybe the town could offer him free water for ten years for payment of the land. Both parties win."

"That's brilliant Henry."

His cheeks tinted pink and she changed her mind

about his looks. He was even more handsome now. Hands down.

"You should feel free to suggest it during negotiations tomorrow."

"You should bring it up. It's your idea."

"I don't care about accolades. I want peace here."

25

He swallowed as they chatted about the water tower and the negotiations tomorrow. He was falling for Everleigh Hayes, and it would be so fucking hard when she left. Unbearably hard.

Inhaling deeply, he slowly navigated the bumpy field as they left the farm. He turned toward his farm and swallowed the enormous lump in his throat.

She watched the scenery as they drove down the road. "Where are we going?"

"My farm."

"Oh. That's nice. But, why?"

"I take possession tomorrow. This place will be filled with people milling about, courtesy of my mom. She's called all of the GHOST folks back home and they're coming with trucks and trailers to take what I don't want. So, tonight, I thought we could have a picnic and solitude on the front porch."

"Oh." He glanced at her and saw her swallow. "That's..." She inhaled. "Lovely."

"I guess I should have asked you if you had something to do. Am I taking you away from something?"

She shook her head and blinked her eyes rapidly. "No." It came out as a whisper. A sweet, whisper.

He turned into the driveway and stopped the truck close to the house. She glanced at the porch and gasped. "When did you get rocking chairs?"

He chuckled. "Today. My parents got them for me. There's also a cooler on the porch with dinner inside. It's likely only sandwiches or something simple, but I figured you'd be hungry."

She turned her head and stared into his eyes. Hers were watery, her nose a cute pink. "That's very thoughtful."

He grinned and nodded. He didn't get that emotional. Nope.

Moving around the front of the truck he helped her down and took her hand in his left hand as he escorted her to the porch. "Take your pick of chairs."

She giggled and took the one to the left. The chairs were shiny black, like she'd suggested, with red cushions on the seat. He pulled the cooler toward them and knelt down to pull the contents of their dinner out. His parents had also purchased a small round table for between the chairs and he set their wrapped sandwiches on the table. He chuckled when he saw a bottle of wine and read the note attached to the neck of the bottle out loud.

"Henry and Everleigh, enjoy your peaceful dinner. Tomorrow, we get to work. Happy Housewarming. Love, Mom and Dad."

"Your parents are so thoughtful."

"They are the best."

She nodded and he noticed the wistful glance over the field. He knew her parents were hands-off and not communicative. It was sad really. They were missing out on a beautiful human being. Smart, sweet, gorgeous. All of the things any man would love in a life partner. All the things he wanted in a life partner.

"My mom said she felt you stiffen up when she hugged you last night."

Her head dropped and she stared at her fingers in her lap for a long time. "She wasn't criticizing, she just noticed and asked if she shouldn't have hugged you."

Everleigh swallowed then her chest rose and fell. "I'm not used to being hugged. My parents did it so seldom that it's weird for me to be hugged by someone I barely know."

He nodded, a knot formed in his stomach as he processed her words.

"My family, biological and family by choice, are huggers. When the women get here tomorrow, you'll likely be hugged a lot. If it will be terribly uncomfortable, I can ask Mom to warn them not to hug you."

A soft smile made that cute little dimple appear. "I'd like to get used to being hugged. I'm conflicted though. When I leave here, I may miss not having people to hug me."

"Maybe you need to stay here for a while longer to absorb those hugs. And, maybe you'll find yourself here."

He rose and sat on his chair and they proceeded to open their sandwiches and eat. He stopped and opened the wine, digging into the cooler once more for glasses. He laughed when he found glass wine glasses. "This is courtesy of my mom, I can assure you. Dad would have packed plastic cups."

She laughed. He poured them each a glass and she held her glass out to him.

"I'd like to make a toast. Henry Delany, congratulations on the purchase of your very own farm. I have no doubt you will make this place flourish and shine. You have support. You have a dream. You have what it takes to make it all happen. Cheers."

"Cheers." It came out a bit shaky. He didn't quite have everything.

They sipped their wine, and ate their sandwiches, then sat back and stared out over the fields. She softly muttered, "This is like a slice of heaven. When you have animals out there to watch, it's going to be amazing."

He reached over and took her hand in his. And they sat like that in the quiet for a long time. Bugs flitted around the weeds, bees and flies and other flying creatures, doing what they do to pollinate and eat. A bird swooped down from overhead to grab a fly in its beak, then flew into the trees. The circle of life.

The sun started its descent, creeping ever closer to the landscape. The color changed, and turned the sky a brilliant orange, fading to yellow.

Everleigh sighed. "Stunning."

"It is."

"This is the stuff dreams are made of."

His thumb brushed her fingers. He was loathe to lose the connection with her so he held her hand. They sat in comfortable silence, looking at his farm, enjoying time with each other. His heart yearned for more of this. With her. With Everleigh. They'd only known each other for a few days, but there was something about her that called to him. He'd never had that weird connection or pull to a woman before, his brain scrambled now to figure out if someone could fall in love this fast. Then he remembered his parents' story of how they met, and he knew it absolutely was possible, even in the worst of times.

The sun had sunk halfway into the earth, and they'd lose all their light in a few minutes. "I hate to say it, but we'll have to go soon."

Her voice was soft when she responded. "I know. Just one more minute?"

"Yeah. One more minute."

She laid her head against the back of the chair and he studied her profile for a long time. Another stupid lump grew in his throat, and he swallowed a few times to get it down.

Finally, she sighed, then began picking up their discarded wrappers, wine glasses, and wine bottle and set them gently into the cooler.

Fastening the lid on top, she stood, stared out at the farm once more, then turned to Henry. "I'm ready."

She was ready, but he wasn't. However, he lifted his body out of the chair. He suddenly felt as though he'd gained a thousand pounds. The weight of the world on his shoulders. Bending to pick up the cooler, he took Everleigh's hand in his, carried the cooler in the other, and they silently strode toward the truck. He was melancholy. He wondered if she was too.

26

Henry pulled into the parking lot of the Homeland Guest House and put the truck in park. "I'd like you to come back to the HOG. Pack your things and come back with me. We'll have protection, and after today with Craig, I don't trust him not to start something. He's already shown his brass."

She swallowed and looked down at her hands in her lap. "I was wondering about that. I don't want to impose."

"You are not an imposition."

"Do you have enough bedrooms?"

"We do. But I have a king-size bed with one side empty."

She chuckled. "And parents in the house."

"Who also know how I feel about you."

"How do they know about..." She swallowed. "How do you feel about me?"

"I have never cared for anyone the way I care for you." She noted the catch in his throat.

She nodded but said nothing.

"What about my car?"

"Let's leave it for now. Tomorrow I can have Flynn's garage come out to fix the tires and bring it to the HOG."

She swallowed the knot in her throat. It was going to hurt so bad when she left. So. Fucking. Bad.

She whispered. "Okay."

They exited the vehicle, and he kept his hand at the small of her back as they walked. But she knew he was watching all around. That was what he did.

Upstairs in her room, she pulled her suitcase from the closet, and began methodically packing as she always did, only this time she wasn't leaving town. Henry sat at the desk and answered emails and texts. She had a system, so she didn't need his help. She was a master at this.

After packing her suitcase, she slid her laptop into her case, and inserted her notebooks inside as well. She tossed her laptop bag over her shoulder, pulled the handle up on her suitcase and grinned. "I'm all set whenever you are."

He turned to face her, his eyes scanned her suitcase, her laptop bag, her purse, and finally her body. His eyes slid up to hers, a grin formed on his lips. "Efficient."

"I've done this a time or two."

He stood, took the suitcase handle from her hands, lifted her laptop bag from her shoulder then held his hand out toward the door. "After you."

She turned on her heels and stepped to the door. Once they'd moved into the hall, he pulled the door closed, then followed her to the elevator.

"Do I check out?"

"No."

"Okay." Her stomach rolled. Why? Was it in case he wanted her gone? Her emotions were a mess right now. She'd need to call her sister this evening if she could.

They stepped into the elevator, and he softly said, "If Craig checks, it looks like you're still here."

Ahh. Her heart raced at that admission and she felt instantly better. What a roller coaster of emotions she was on.

The ride to the HOG was reasonably short. She barely had time to get her thoughts together before he pulled into the garage.

"This was an old factory?"

"Yeah. A sewing factory. GHOST completely renovated the first level last year for us. Now they're in the middle of renovating the upstairs to make way for babies."

"Oh, right. Lara and Tate's baby."

"And, I imagine one day Spencer and Kenna will start having babies. So, we have the space, we want to use it."

"Smart."

Tapping the garage door closed, he grinned then stepped out of the truck. He hurried around to the passenger side and helped her down. Then pulled her suitcase and laptop bag from the backseat.

Her stomach flipped and rolled. She'd be meeting everyone at the same time. At least those she hadn't met. And, Hawk and Roxanne would know for sure she and Henry were sleeping together as soon as they retire for the night. How would they feel about that? If she were a mom, how would she feel about her son sleeping with a woman, he'd recently met? If she could articulate her feelings for Henry, she'd reassure them that she cared for him deeply. But they also knew she'd be leaving after negotiations were over. They'd worry about him getting hurt. She worried about herself getting hurt. There was no perfect scenario for this situation.

Henry opened the door and ushered her inside. Tate,

Lara, Myles, and his parents were at the table playing cards.

Roxanne stood. "Hi, you two. So great to see you."

She strode across the floor and hugged Henry. Then Roxanne wrapped her arms around her and squeezed. It was a genuine hug. It felt good. It brought tears to her eyes. When had her mother last hugged her? She vaguely remembered a day when she was in third grade and had won the national spelling bee. Surely there'd been other times since then, but she couldn't recall them. Usually, only when she'd done something worth celebrating. Never upon walking into the room. She forced herself to relax in Roxanne's arms. Then she tightened her hold on Roxanne, hoping to convey things she didn't know how to say.

Henry announced, "I brought Everleigh back here because things got heated with Craig this afternoon."

"Oh, no. What happened?"

"He lunged at Everleigh, and I dropped him with a right."

Tate clapped his hands, Lara joined him. His father chuckled and his mom grabbed his right hand and looked it over. "Are you alright?"

"A little sore, but it was worth it."

"Henry."

He shook his head. Leaning down he kissed his mom's head, then said again. "Totally worth it."

His father leaned back in his chair. "I can't wait to hear about it."

"Let me get Everleigh settled, then we'll come out and chat."

His dad began shuffling the cards. Henry tilted his head toward the bedroom and began rolling her suitcase.

Once in his room, he closed the door. "I have room in my closet. I'll make room in my drawers while you hang your clothes. My bathroom is through that door..." He pointed to a room at the back. "Make yourself comfortable."

He opened a drawer and began moving clothing around. She silently began hanging her meager clothing. She bought nice clothing because she could afford it. And the expensive clothing wore well and didn't wrinkle as bad. But it was pitiful that all her clothing fit in a large suitcase. It was a source of embarrassment as she looked upon her life. Everything she owned fit in a large suitcase.

Henry walked into the bathroom and opened and closed drawers while she put her workout clothing and her undergarments in the drawers he'd made room in. She lined her shoes up in the closet near his, then took her toiletry bag into the bathroom. Henry grinned. "I managed a drawer."

"That's perfect. Thank you."

27

Oh, his heart hammered in his chest, and he imagine this was what it was like to be in love. He'd never been in love, and he'd never felt like this before. So, by process of elimination, he thought he must be.

Everleigh exited the bathroom looking nervous and yet simply stunning. He held his arms open and she eagerly walked into his embrace. His heartbeat was strong and rapid. He laid his cheek on the top of her head.

She chuckled, "Your heart is beating so fast."

"It is."

Her arms tightened around his waist. "Mine is too."

His eyes closed and he concentrated on the feeling of her against his body and her scent. He'd remember how she felt against him forever.

After a few moments he pulled away, plastered on a smile and said, "Shall we go visit?"

"We should."

They entered the kitchen to laughter and Myles declaring his third win. Tate told him it was still a tie and they broke each other's balls a bit. Hawk turned, "Henry, get me a beer, please."

Tate called out, "Me, too."

Henry grabbed two beers from the refrigerator and handed them to Everleigh. "What do you want?" She peered inside and spotted the hard seltzer. "I'll take one of those please."

Nodding, he grabbed a seltzer, then turned to the table. "Mom, Lara, do you need anything?"

Lara laughed, "Nothing for me."

His mom smiled and held up her wine glass. He dutifully filled her glass and sat at the table next to Everleigh.

His dad stopped shuffling cards. "Let's hear about this altercation."

Tate chuckled. "And don't leave any details out about Craig going down. I want to hear it all."

He proceeded to tell them about their afternoon. They laughed and clapped their hands when he told them about his encounter with Craig.

Tate shook his head. "I know we shouldn't laugh, but that asshole has had it coming for a long time. I simply don't know what he'll do once control is firmly taken from him. I think he'll either have to leave, which I kind of hate to think of, because we can't keep tabs on him. Or, in jail where he'd be under lock and key. That's really the best place for him."

Henry laughed. "I think you're right."

His phone rang and he saw Adelaide's name on his screen. "It's Addy." Tapping his phone, "Hey, Addy, what's up?"

"So, there's a woman from the mountain who snuck down here. She wants to talk to Everleigh. She's scared. She seems sincere and she's afraid to be seen down here."

"Okay. We're at the HOG. It'll be about ten minutes."

Hanging up he looked at Everleigh. "There's a woman from the mountain who snuck down to see you. Addy says she's scared but it's important to talk to you."

"Oh." Everleigh stood. "I can go."

"Not alone."

"You don't have to interrupt your time with your family."

He stood and huffed out a breath. "Everleigh, I'm your protection."

"Oh."

He glanced at his parents. "We'll be back as soon as we can."

Tate called out, "If you need help, call."

"Addy and Maya are there. They're as badass as they come."

Tate laughed. Myles responded. "Truth."

He ushered Everleigh to the bedroom where she grabbed her purse. "I won't bring my laptop. I don't know what she wants."

"That's fine. I can't imagine either."

They hurried from the room and through the kitchen. The instant they were buckled in the truck he headed them toward the construction site where Addy and Maya were on duty.

As he drove, his mind raced. What on earth could she want, and was this a diversion that could harm Everleigh?

He tapped the call icon on his steering wheel. "Hey, there."

"Addy. You don't think she's a diversion for something Craig has planned, do you?"

"We thought about that. Maya is out doing a sweep right now. I'm watching her on camera."

"Where's the woman?"

"She's hiding in the woods. She won't come out."

"How did she make contact with you?"

"I was doing a sweep and she tossed pebbles from the woods. I called out to whoever it was and she whispered that she couldn't be seen. I told her I wasn't coming in there without some proof she was alone. She stepped to the edge of the woods and walked a distance along the road out of sight. We chatted across the road."

"And you believe her?"

"We both feel her fear is genuine. Whether it's fear that Craig will punish her if she doesn't do this or if he'll punish her if he finds out are both different fears. In the dark and without backup, we can't tell. But our job is to protect the base right now. That's why I called, plus she specifically said Everleigh's name."

He glanced at Everleigh, who listened intently but said nothing. "Okay. Almost there."

He disconnected the call and drove into the construction site and to the office. Addy walked out and a few moments later, Maya came from the back of the construction site.

"Let's go into the office to talk this out."

Upon entering the office, Henry grinned. "Everleigh Hayes, meet Maya Sager and Adelaide Masters. Ladies, Everleigh Hayes."

Everleigh shook both of their hands, smiling as she did. She then began the conversation. "So, she asked for me. You know she's afraid, but are unsure the direction of her fear."

Maya nodded. "Yes. And, while I did a perimeter sweep again, I tossed rocks into the woods along the way to see if anyone moved or ran. Other than a bird or two, there was no movement."

Henry looked at the cameras on the computer screens in the office. "Show me where she is. I think Everleigh and I will get into the truck and drive to her. She'll be hidden and Everleigh will be safe. If Craig is planning something, I'll take off."

Maya and Addy both nodded. Addy said, "That works. Put on a comm unit."

Henry pulled one from a box in a locker they kept inside the office. "Comm on," he said. Both women gave him a thumbs-up.

Turning to Everleigh he nodded. "You don't get out of the truck. You don't open the door, no matter what she says. Got it?"

"Yes."

"I'm serious, Everleigh. No matter what."

"I understand."

He ushered her to the truck once again and drove to the spot where the woman was supposedly hiding.

He turned the truck so he could take off if needed and lowered his window.

28

Her heart raced. This was the kind of stuff she wasn't at all used to. She negotiated situations that weren't quite so contentious. Usually, people grumbled about land or possessions. That's what she'd been negotiating for years. This was a new one in her line of work, and it was wearing on her. In some ways, she was getting sick and tired of listening to people whine and complain that someone else got Grandma's sewing machine and china collection. Families ruined themselves over stupid, nonsensical stuff. Buy another sewing machine, sew your ass off, and make Grandma proud. Fighting over something that wasn't going to bring her back and destroyed your family in the process was idiotic. People who had family and pushed them away didn't understand the yearning one felt for a close family.

Tears sprang to her eyes. She'd just had an awakening. It just now dawned on her that she longed for a close family. How to get it? That was the question.

Light tapping against Henry's truck caused him to swear. "Dammit. Don't throw rocks at my truck."

"Sorry." A soft voice called out.

"Step into the light," he boomed.

A frail, pale woman stepped from the trees on Everleigh's side of the truck. Her eyes darted to and fro, her shoulders slumped slightly, her posture was curved. She wore a brown cloak, older and patched. She had a brown scarf on her head, the hair that could be seen was graying.

Everleigh rolled her window down and Henry reminded her, "Do not step out or open the door."

"I won't."

She called out to the woman, "Can you come any closer?"

The woman's head turned toward the mountain, then she stepped one step closer to the truck.

"I'm Everleigh Hayes. I understand you asked to talk to me."

"Promise you won't tell." Her voice was soft. A tinge of shaking could be heard.

"I promise."

"He's going crazy. He's destroying our homes and things. We don't have much but he's in a rage. They're trying to control him, but he's unhinged. Please get him and put him in jail. Please stop this. Please, I beg you."

"Where is Gerard?"

"Craig beat him pretty bad. Liliana, his wife, is tending to him. Jasiah and some others are out searching for Craig now. He stalked off down the other side of the mountain. I don't trust him. We don't know where he is."

"I'll do what I can. Do you have a place you can go to be safe?"

"I only have here."

Everleigh turned to him and Henry shook his head.

"But..."

"We can't. The only thing I could do is call the sheriff and see if they can take her to the jail for protection."

Everleigh turned to the woman. "Do you want us to do that?"

The woman's eyes watered. Finally, she nodded. "Yes. Please."

Henry dialed the sheriff's department and the deputy on duty said he was on his way. As they waited, Everleigh tried to calm the woman. "You aren't going to jail because you did anything wrong. They'll take you to a safe house where you can stay and be safe for the night. Hopefully, Jasiah will find Craig soon. We won't tell anyone you spoke to us."

The woman nodded but said nothing. Sirens grew closer just as the woman turned to run. Everleigh called out to her. "Wait. Don't go."

The woman crouched down near the road. Everleigh's heart broke for this woman. Even with her own lack of family, and now knowing she wanted one desperately, she'd never been afraid to go home. She just didn't have a home.

The sheriff's deputy stopped near Henry's truck and Henry jumped out with a look toward her to stay put. He stood in front of his truck and asked the woman to come out. She glanced at the mountain, then looked to Everleigh. Everleigh swallowed the knot that had formed as she watched this woman process fear, and nodded.

Henry hunched down and softly said, "If you want us to make it look like you're being arrested so if Craig is watching, he'll think we took you instead of you contacting us, we can do that."

The woman swallowed then slowly stood. "No, I can

walk myself. My daddy would be so sad if he thought I got arrested."

Henry smiled. "How old is your daddy?"

"He's sixty-two. I've always tried to be good and not cause trouble. I'd hate to start now."

Henry chuckled and as she watched him escort the woman to the squad car, her heart grew so big she thought it would burst out of her chest. She laid her right hand against her heart as the tears slipped down her cheeks.

"Oh, my god." She whispered. "Oh, my god. I love him."

Gathering her emotions, she inhaled some deep breaths and swiped at the tears that had fallen. She watched the three chat and the woman turned to her and nodded before climbing in the backseat of the squad. Everleigh waved to her and tried to implant in her brain to ask the sheriff what her name was.

Henry climbed into the truck and Everleigh turned to him. "Thank you."

He scoffed. "Thank you. She wanted you."

"But you helped her, too."

He grinned and shrugged his right shoulder. "I guess we're a good team."

Ouch. Yes. But, ouch. That hit her right in the heart and if she said a word right now, she'd burst out crying for sure.

Instead she nodded and he pulled out onto the county road.

"How about we drive a bit before going back?"

"Yeah. That would be great."

He turned down a farm road not far from his place and just as they'd passed a run-down looking barn a horse ran out onto the road. Henry slammed on his brakes and jumped from the truck. She followed him.

Just as she got out a man with a long stick in his hand came flying out of the field screaming, "Come back here you no good fucker."

29

Henry grabbed the switch from the man's hand and shoved him to the road. "Are you beating that horse?"

"That's none of your goddam business."

"The hell it isn't. You don't beat horses."

"Maybe you don't, you do-gooder, but when the fuckers don't listen to me, I do."

The man stood and tried grabbing the switch from him, and Henry decided to give him a piece of his own medicine. He slapped that switch across the man's backside, and he howled.

"You motherfucker."

"Sit your ass down." He was as mad as he'd ever been. To beat an animal was total bullshit.

"I don't have to listen to you."

"The fuck you don't." He snapped him again with the switch, then pushed the man to the ground near the edge of the ditch. He turned to find Everleigh standing a few feet from the horse talking to it. Her voice was calm and the horse, though its breathing was still heavy, its ears twitched at her voice.

Everleigh sat at the edge of the road and kept talking to the horse. Its head bobbed up and down a few times, then it took a step toward her. Everleigh continued to talk to the horse, and he stood mesmerized as she calmed this poor beaten beast with just her voice.

Every time the farmer opened his mouth Henry raised the switch, which shut him up. But, also, every time the farmer said anything, the horse flinched and shook.

Everleigh continued talking to the horse. It took more than thirty minutes for it to trust her enough to come over and sniff her. She slowly held her hand out, palm up and the horse sniffed her. Ever so slowly, she rolled her hand, and petted the horse's nose. They spent time with each other and finally Everleigh stood. She stayed in one place, allowing the horse to trust her movements, then the horse came to her once again. It had a bridle on, and so very slowly, Everleigh took the bridle in her hand and walked the horse down the road. She looked back at him, nodding to the farmer and he took that as *get him out*.

He bit out, "Stand up and walk to your house, very slowly or you'll get the switch."

"I don't have to listen to you."

"Yes, you do."

"I'll call the sheriff."

"I'll save you the call." The farmer stood, though he huffed and puffed as if he was the one inconvenienced. Henry followed him, though he grumbled and swore, as Henry tapped the sheriff's number.

"Glen Hollow Sheriff's Department."

"It's Henry Delany again. I need someone out at..." He nudged the farmer. "What's your name?"

"Fuck you."

"I know where you're at Henry. You're out at Case Evan's place. I'll be right out."

"Seems you're on a first name basis with the sheriff. Good to know." Henry quipped as he tucked his phone into his pocket.

"Fuck you."

"Limited vocabulary, too."

"Fuck you." Only this time it was a mumble.

Henry chuckled. Fucker.

As soon as they made it down the long driveway, the sheriff's squad came down the road. No sirens, just lights. He pulled down the driveway and right behind him, he saw Everleigh walking down the driveway with the horse alongside her.

She walked the horse toward the barn and he nodded to the deputy. "Caught him beating this horse."

"I didn't beat it."

Henry grabbed him by the scruff and dragged him to the barn. He tried to get away, but Henry was pissed. There's no way he'd let this asshole get away now. Inside, Everleigh turned the lights on, and the horse's backside was welted. Everleigh gasped and the farmer muttered a string of expletives. The horse grew agitated and Everleigh tried calming her down.

Henry turned to the deputy, "Can you put him in the car so the horse can calm down?"

"My pleasure."

Deputy Gordon dragged Case Evans toward the squad car, and Henry moved toward Everleigh. She turned and smiled. "If you could close the door and sit over there on a bale of hay, that would be helpful."

He stared into her eyes a moment, then turned and

did as she asked. The hay poked into his slacks, but he was mesmerized watching Everleigh. She let go of the bridle and sat on a bale of hay. The horse paced a bit, back and forth, but Everleigh sat perfectly still. She turned and saw a bag of feed. Reaching in, she pulled a handful of corn from inside. She held her hand out, palm up, filled with feed, and after a few moments, the horse came to her. It gently nibbled then stepped away. Then came forward and nibbled, then stepped away. Everleigh spoke to her constantly. "You are so beautiful. You are loved. I love you. You are magnificent. I'll take care of you. Together, we'll conquer the world, you and I."

The horse bobbed its head up and down as if it understood her. After a while, she stood and found a bucket. She filled the bucket with corn and strode to him. He scooted to the side of his bale of hay, and she sat next to him. The bucket of corn between them. She pulled out another handful of corn and held it out.

Softly she said, "You do the same. It may take some time for her to trust you. You're a man and she's been beaten by a man."

"Okay." He filled his hand and held it out. The horse nodded and moved back and forth, unsure of what to do. Everleigh giggled. "It's okay. I trust him."

The horse's head bobbed high and low. Finally, she made some progress toward them. Everleigh noticed other horses in stalls beginning to poke their heads out to see what was going on.

She laughed. "Oh, look how pretty they all are."

He chuckled at her enthusiasm and leaned over and kissed the side of her head. "You are a beautiful human, Everleigh."

She turned and stared into his eyes. "So are you, Henry."

He leaned down and kissed her lips. Softly. Gently. Then she giggled. The horse had neared and was eating out of her hand. Not his. Not yet. But he'd work towards it.

"How are you so good with them?"

"I learned about horses as a girl growing up. I'll tell you about it one day."

The deputy entered the barn a few moments later and the horse ran to the other end of the barn. "We've been called out here a few times. He always gets these horses back. Sadly, until we can put him in jail for cruelty, he claims its discipline and they are returned to him."

"I'll see about that."

He stalked out toward the squad car and opened the door on the opposite side of the car where Case sat. Henry assessed his age to be late forties.

"I'll make you a deal. I'll buy these horses from you, and you never buy a horse, or a dog, or a cat or any animal ever again and I won't come after you."

"Oh, are you threatening me?"

"Call it what you want. But I'll buy your stock, your feed and some of your equipment and you wash your hands of animals. You aren't cut out for animals."

"Fuck you."

"Right. Maybe you can get some English lessons too."

The sheriff approached and Henry turned to him. "I'll buy his animals and his feed. I don't want him owning animals ever again."

"That's a great plan, but you'll have to get him to agree."

"How about a couple nights in jail? My mom is an

attorney, and I'll have her make a visit to him tomorrow. She's very persuasive."

Deputy Gordon chuckled. "I'd love to see that." He slammed the door. "I can hold him on a cooldown period. I can only hold him for three days without charging him."

"We'll get it done in three days. Does he have family?"

"Nope. His wife left a few years ago and they didn't have children."

"Blessing there. Everleigh and I will stay here with the animals and make sure they are taken care of until we work out a deal."

Deputy Gordon shook his head. "You're one of a kind, Henry."

"She's one of a kind." He pointed to the barn and Deputy Gordon chuckled and got into the car.

30

She looked the horse over and saw the welts on her backside. Tears welled in her eyes. She was beautiful, why would anyone beat on her? She strolled past the other stalls and petted those who weren't afraid of her. The others she spoke to softly and moved on. They'd get used to her.

The barn door opened and Henry strode in. His eyes sought hers and her heartbeat kicked up a notch. It always did. She stood still, not wanting to scare the horses.

"There are seven of them. They've all been beaten. The one in the back stall..." She pointed to the end of the barn, "Has cuts that should be looked at."

Henry nodded and pulled her to his body. His arms wrapped around her and squeezed her tightly and she'd never felt safer and happier.

He kissed the top of her head and stepped back. "I'm going to buy them."

"Buy them." She looked into his eyes. "The horses? You're going to buy them?"

"I am. I asked him, he said 'fuck you', which seems to

be all he can say. But Deputy Gordon is taking him to jail for three days. I'll have my mom visit him tomorrow. You've met her. She can smile and speak to him like she's doing him a favor, and I'll own the horses and the feed."

She choked back a sob and jumped into his arms. The horse jumped and whinnied, hopefully she understood, but likely not. Henry held her for a few moments. Kissed her like she'd never been kissed before. And slowly let her slide down his body.

"That's fantastic."

"I told Deputy Gordon we'd stay here tonight. I'm going to have my dad bring us sleeping bags, water, and food and we'll bed down in a stall. I don't want to go into his house. We can go home tomorrow to shower. We'll stay with them until we have permission to take them to my farm."

She squeezed him tightly. After a while, she tilted her head to look into his eyes. "I love you, Henry Delany."

His hand cupped her jaw, and his eyes delved into hers. "I love you, Everleigh Hayes." His head dipped and his lips touched hers and it was like magic. True magic.

They stood together for a long time, which was good, because her knees shook. She'd never declared her love before. No one had ever told her they loved her. Except her sister. But that was totally different. Everleigh Hayes was a thirty-year-old woman who finally, finally found love.

Something pushed her back and she stumbled into Henry. He chuckled and she turned to see her horse staring at her.

She laid her hand against the horse's jaw. "Aww, are you jealous? He's good. I promise you, he'll never, ever hit you. If he ever would, I'd make him pay."

Henry laughed. "I bet you would, too."

The horse's head bobbed in understanding. At least she thought it was. And Henry chuckled. "I'll call Dad."

He walked to the end of the barn and pulled his phone out. She heard his voice softly explaining to his dad what had just happened, and she petted her new horse and visited the others. She wanted to call a veterinarian but thought she should talk to Henry first. After all, she might be overstepping. But she had the money to pay, and she'd surely get this poor baby some care.

She stepped to the stall to her right and looked in at the beautiful bay mare looking at her with fear in her eyes and as she stared at her new friend, the other horse nudged her way in beside her and neighed. The horse in the stall bobbed its head in understanding and slowly approached. She knelt down and grabbed some feed for her newest friend and giggled when she fed from her hand. Her ribs were prominent, these poor souls likely didn't eat nearly enough.

She inhaled to calm herself. There would likely be many days like this to come. Sadness for all these animals had endured. They reminded her of the woman from the mountain. Life sucked sometimes.

Henry approached slowly. "Dad will be here soon. I suspect Mom will be with him."

"Do they have sleeping bags and stuff?"

He chuckled. "Baby, we go out on missions all the time. You'll be amazed at how we're set up."

"Oh. I hadn't thought of that."

His arm wrapped around her shoulders, but her horse friend nudged it off and he laughed. "She loves you. But not as much as I do."

Aww. "I love her too." She lowered her voice. "But not more than you."

The horse in the stall bobbed its head and she laughed.

"Henry, the horse in the end stall needs veterinary care. Do you know who I can call? I'll pay for it."

"You don't need to pay for it. I will. Let me call Lara. She's lived here most of her life."

He spoke to Lara and she reflected again, for the thousandth time, just today, how lucky she was to have met him.

Her phone chimed and she looked down to see an email from Casper. "I have the new job set up for you in North Carolina when you are finished in Glen Hollow. Please update me as to your progress."

Her heart sank. Tears sprang to her eyes immediately. It was time to leave. Almost time to leave.

Her breathing came in short spurts and she felt like she'd pass out. She slumped down to a bale of hay and prayed her heart would hold out and not break into tiny shards never to be fully bonded together. Finally gaining control, she sat upright. The barn door opened, and Hawk and Roxanne entered. Their smiles were huge.

Roxanne went first to Henry and hugged him, then walked toward her. She braced herself for a hug, reminded herself it was a good thing. As soon as Roxanne's arms were around her shoulders, she burst out crying.

Roxanne held her tight and whispered in her ear. "It's okay honey. It's okay. Whatever I can do, I'll help you."

But could she?

31

Henry turned his attention to Everleigh and his mom. What was she crying about?

His dad leaned in, "It's been a rather emotional day. You two have had a lot going on."

"Yeah." But she'd been fine a minute ago.

His dad nudged him. "I've got supplies in the truck. Are you sure you want to stay here in the barn? You could always get up early and come out here."

"I know. But, if the horses are going to get used to me, I want to make the effort by staying with them and protecting them."

"I get it. I'm proud of you, son."

His heartbeat kicked up. He'd always wanted his parents to be proud of him. "Thanks, Dad." He swallowed as they walked to the truck. "I love her."

His dad glanced at him. "I suspected so."

"Why?" His steps faltered slightly.

"The way you look at her. It's plain to see."

He nodded. He hadn't thought about that. He could always tell how much his dad loved his mom by the way he looked at her. His expression changed when he looked at his mom. He must have inherited that. Hopefully, Everleigh saw it too.

"Have you talked about what happens when her job is over?"

A hard, dry lump formed in his stomach. His throat constricted and the word was coarse when it came out. "No."

"I think you should."

"I know."

His dad pulled the tailgate open, and they each grabbed armloads of supplies and carried them to the barn.

When they entered, his mom and Everleigh sat on a bale of hay near the far end of the barn. The horse that loved Everleigh nudged her every time she stopped petting her. He grinned. She was a horse whisperer.

His mom held out a handful of feed and the horse leaned over and licked some of it up. Both women giggled and his heart grew another few inches. He'd have no room left in his chest at this rate.

He looked around the empty stalls. There were two. Both were surprisingly clean. But he pulled the twine off a bale of hay and laid new hay on the ground in the stall. His dad grabbed a large wool blanket from a pack and opened that up and spread it over the hay. Then he dug around for something while Henry opened the two sleeping bags and laid them on top of the blanket. He chuckled. "I've never slept in a barn before."

His dad chuckled. "I have a few times on missions. It was a great place to stay out of the elements. Though, I'll say, they weren't as clean as this one."

His dad pulled a cooler into the stall. "You have water,

cheese, and a couple of drinks in here. Since you didn't get to finish yours tonight at the HOG, we figured you'd want a couple. Lara packed some food and cookies too. They are in the covered container. Come home in the morning for breakfast."

He hugged his dad. "Thanks, Dad. We appreciate it."

"We know."

He turned and saw his mom and Everleigh chatting, so he sauntered toward them. His mom turned and smiled brightly at him. "So what do I need to do tomorrow?"

"You need to visit Case Evans in jail in the morning and explain how very beneficial it would be to him to sell these horses and feed to me. I'll look around in the morning at the equipment and see what I'll need at my farm. Right now, I think I may need to buy the hay from his field too. Before you go, I'll text you a list."

"I can do that."

He chuckled. "I know you can. He's all pissy tonight, but I'm hoping a night in jail will calm him down. Also, I'd like the purchase agreement to state he agrees to never own animals again. He's not a man who should own animals. They don't deserve his kind of care."

His mom chuckled and stood. She hugged him tightly and he closed his eyes and absorbed her love. His mom whispered in his ear, "You and Everleigh need to talk about the future."

"I know."

She squeezed once more and stood back. She hugged Everleigh, then stood back and looked into her eyes. "Okay?"

Everleigh nodded and smiled.

His mom nodded once, then turned to his dad. "Let's

go big man. This old woman's getting tired. And we have a big day tomorrow."

His dad chuckled, waved, and put his arm around his mom's shoulders. "You're not a day older than the day I met you." He kissed the top of her head and escorted her out of the barn.

He held his hand out to Everleigh, relief flooded him when she put her hand in his. Her horse, though, seemed a bit irritated. He chuckled. "What shall we do with this one tonight?"

"I think her stall is right here." She pointed to a stall across from them. "And according to the name scribbled on the stall door, her name is Harper. But I think she looks like a Sallie."

"I think we can change her name. The old one likely comes with some pain."

"I hadn't thought of that. But we could start calling her by her current name with kindness and erase the pain."

He turned to face her. Leaning forward he kissed her forehead. "You are the sweetest person I've ever met."

She sighed. Then she looked up at him. "Did Lara know a veterinarian?"

"She did. I have the number of Dr. Emily Zsidai. I'll call her now and explain what we have. If she thinks she should be looked at tonight, then I'd like to let her come out. Is that alright with you?"

"Yes. Please."

He tapped the text from Lara and then the number for Dr. Zsidai. "Dr. Emily."

"Hello, Dr. Emily. My name is Henry Delany, my girlfriend and I are out at the Evans' farm."

"Oh, dear."

"So you've been called out here before?"

"Sadly. What happened?"

"We have a horse here with open welts. I'm not sure if there's something we can do until morning or if you need to see her right away."

"I'll come right away so infection doesn't set in. It'll take me about fifteen minutes to get to you."

"We'll be here."

He pocketed his phone, took Everleigh's hand and sauntered to a bale of hay near their stall. "I think we need to have a talk."

32

They did. They absolutely did.

"I agree."

"Dr. Emily will be here in fifteen minutes. We can start our discussion now or wait."

"We can start now. I got an email. Casper has another job for me."

His shoulders slumped and it seemed as though his eyes watered. Hers did just saying that out loud.

"Are you taking it?"

Her head jerked up. No one had ever asked her that question before. She'd never considered that she could take a job or not. "I haven't responded. Can I say no?"

"Yes. You can say no."

"But what would I do? I have money saved, but eventually I'll have to make more."

"I'm going to have seven horses to take care of. They're afraid of me, but not of you. You have a way with them. Stay with me. Live with me. Take care of the horses. Get them healthy. Once they're healthy we'll see about breeding them or what we can do to make money with them."

"But, in the meantime I won't be earning my keep."

"I just said, they're afraid of me. Of men. I need to rehab them. You can do that. Life is more than about 'earning your keep'. Of course, there are living expenses and we have to work to keep a roof over our heads and food on the table. But you've been a workaholic your entire life. There's more to life. You need to start living it. Figure out what Everleigh likes to do in her spare time. That means actually having spare time."

"But I've never not made money. I've never..."

"Everleigh, I make good money. I have money in a trust fund that I've barely touched. We'll be fine. You'll have a home. A real home. And I'll have you. We'll be together and see if we like that."

A knocking sounded on the door then it creaked open. "I'm Dr. Emily."

Her heart stuttered in her chest. Her breathing came in short hard bursts. She could have a home. With Henry. With this man she loved and who loved her.

Henry leaned forward and held his hand out to Dr. Emily. "Henry Delany. This is Everleigh Hayes."

"Hello, Everleigh. Please tell me what happened here."

She swallowed and plastered on a smile. "The horse I'm most worried about is this one down here." She stumbled toward the stall. Her feet felt like they had lead in them. Her parents would call her lazy and unpracticed if she stayed with Henry and didn't make money and be self-sufficient.

"Oh, goodness." Dr. Emily mumbled. She slowly opened the stall door and slid inside. "Hey there, Queen.

I'm sorry to have to be out here again." She softly spoke to the scared horse and touched her on her neck. Her hand smoothed over Queenie's neck slowly. No jerky movements, just gentle touch and soft speaking. Queen raised and lowered her head as if she'd been through this routine before. It took some time, but Queen finally relaxed enough that Dr. Emily could look at the wounds. After taking a look at them, she opened her bag and pulled out a tube of salve.

"This will help promote healing and keep flies and other bugs from laying eggs in the wounds. You'll need to apply this daily. Sometimes twice each day until healing begins. Do you know when these wounds occurred?"

"No." She sadly shook her head. "We came upon Mr. Evans beating Harper." She motioned to Harper standing nearby watching. "He's in jail right now and we're taking care of the animals until Henry can buy them."

Dr. Emily's brows rose in the air. "I'd love to see that happen. Evans is a monster."

"Yes. We agree."

She glanced at Henry who stood by quietly, sadness in his eyes. They needed to finish their conversation. Her stomach felt as though she'd empty its contents soon. Her chest was so tight, her heart could barely beat.

Dr. Emily continued. "Anyway. Keep the ointment on it. Keep her wounds clean. Only use water to rinse any dirt off. If you have to lightly wipe it, use a clean wet cloth and don't rub hard. It'll be sore for a while but luckily this does have a bit of a numbing agent in it to keep the animals from itching or scratching it. You'll need to keep her from doing that. It's recommended that you take her for walks each day, but don't let her out to pasture because she'll rub herself on a tree and open her wounds. Bring her back into her stall until she heals."

"Okay. I will." She watched Dr. Emily work with Queen. She was gentle and kind. "I noticed some of these horses look a bit malnourished. How much food should they have each day?"

"I'll write out all the instructions for you before I leave. If you buy these horses, where will you take them?"

Henry cleared his throat. "I just purchased the DeWitt Farm. Perry DeWitt."

"Oh, I heard that had sold. That's wonderful. I hear the house is loaded with antiques."

"It has its share, that's for sure."

"Well, good for you. It's a great house, though Perry hasn't managed to keep it up as it should be. But I'm sure you'll make it the grand place it used to be. And these horses will have a better life. They all come from great bloodlines. I think at one point Case thought he'd breed them. But he's not much of a farmer and he couldn't afford stud fees and one thing led to another and his temper got in the way. In healthy condition, these ladies will bring you beautiful foals that will sell high."

Henry nodded. His eyes darted to hers and his brows lifted slightly.

She smiled but turned her attention to Dr. Emily. "I know you're busy, but will you be able to come out again tomorrow and look the rest of these horses over to gauge their health? If we need to add supplements or anything to their diets, I'd like to select correctly."

Dr. Emily smiled brightly. "I'd be happy to help these ladies out. And both of you, of course."

Dr. Emily finished for the evening, wrote out explicit instructions of the proper care and feeding of the horses, and a promise to come back tomorrow to examine each of them. She even said it would be free of charge because she was so happy the horses would be out of Case's care. Such that it was.

And, now they were alone and their talk would resume.

33

He closed the barn door. Locked it up the best he could as Everleigh led Harper to her stall. She petted Harper one last time and softly said, "Good night."

She turned to him and he held his hand out. "Let's go finish our conversation."

"Okay."

He led her to their stall for the night. "Oh, this looks great."

"My dad said he's had to sleep in barns on missions. This is a first for me."

"It's a first for me too." She giggled. "It's kind of fun though."

He turned the lights off but used one of the lanterns his parents brought to light his way to the stall. Everleigh had opened a sleeping bag and was laying on her side, head in hand, facing him when he stepped in. He pulled his boots off, slid into his sleeping bag and faced her. He pulled her free hand toward him and whispered.

"I've never loved a woman before. You're the first."

"I've never loved a man before either. It's all so new."

"It is. I know this is a big decision, Everleigh. But you've already said you don't necessarily love your job. You long for a home. You'll have one with me. But my house won't be a home without you in it. I want a home with you."

"I want a home with you too. It's all so much and yet, it seems completely stupid to even have a hesitation about it. All I can think is what my parents will think of me. They'll call me lazy...."

"They clearly don't know you."

She was quiet but stared into his eyes for a long time. "No. They don't. Not really."

"Why were you crying when my mom hugged you?"

Tears sprang to her eyes, and she cleared her throat gently. "Earlier today when we first arrived at the HOG, your mom got up and hugged you. Just by way of greeting, she hugged you. I tried remembering the last time my mom hugged me and the only time I could remember was when I won a spelling bee when I was nine."

His stomach constricted. This woman hadn't known parental love. Not really. She was fed and housed and taken care of. But she wasn't truly loved. "That's so sad I don't have words."

"Did you grow up with your mom hugging you all the time?"

"I did. My dad too. Big, burly Hawk. Loved his children and his wife and he still does."

A lone tear slid down her cheek and he swiped it away. "I'll hug you every day."

She chuckled.

"I mean it. Every. Single. Day. You'll know my love."

More tears. His nose began tingling and his eyes

watered. But he laid perfectly still, afraid to break the moment.

"When your mom hugged me, it was right after I thought about my last hug from my mom, and then the email I had gotten from Casper about the next job. I couldn't believe I was already going to have to say good-bye. Because I'm not ready. But I have always worked. I need to be independent in some way. It's been drilled into me since birth, I think."

"You know my mom is an independent woman. She's always worked as an attorney, before she met my father and after. He's had to go away on missions and our house ran just like it did when Dad was home. She made money, but it wasn't the topic of conversation because so did he. And they both make great money. We've been comfortable always. But she found a way to be independent with us. And that doesn't mean that she never took time off. She did. Obviously when we were born, she had to. And, when I was around six or seven and Stella was three or four, Mom took a leave of absence from work because she wanted to. It didn't change her independence. And my dad never made her feel like she was beholden to him for a single thing. I think he liked it better when she was home though. He loved walking in the house from a mission and we were all there. He'd been single for a long time before Mom, and once he had a family, that's all he wanted."

He lifted her hand and kissed her fingers. "I will never make you feel like you aren't independent of me. You are who you are Everleigh Hayes. Staying with me. Living with me shouldn't and won't take your independence away. You'll still have it. And if a day comes that raising horses doesn't keep you satisfied, you can go back to negotiating, or whatever it is you think you'll prefer. We'll manage the change together. I know how to do that. I have great role models."

She leaned forward and kissed his lips. His heart beat so fast he figured she could feel it in his lips.

"I'd like to stay with you."

Tears fell, but this time they were his. And hers. And they blended together as he kissed her lips again.

When they pulled slightly apart, he said, "You know, maybe we can make a living out of rehabbing abused animals. You have a way about you. We can get these gals healthy and breed them and make money, and we can bring others in here and there as needed. Dr. Emily is likely the person to speak to about helping out in that area."

"I had been wondering about that. I don't know if my heart will break too much every time I see an abused animal. But, to help them out of a bad situation would surely help it heal."

"I'll help you. With all of it. I'm with GHOST right now, but in the future if I'm needed at home more and we're making money, I can quit GHOST. I love it, and my team-mates, or I can take fewer and fewer missions."

"It does seem like we have options."

For the first time in a long time his smile was genuine. "We do."

34

S he woke to snorting. She laid against Henry, they'd zipped their sleeping bags together. His arm was her pillow. He didn't have one.

She rubbed her eyes and yawned, then heard snorting again.

She looked up and giggled. Henry opened his eyes and looked in the direction she now stared. Harper had somehow gotten out of her stall and was staring in at them.

"Good morning, Harper. How are you today?"

Harper bobbed her head up and down and snorted once more. Everleigh giggled.

Henry unzipped their sleeping bags, and she sat up. He stood, then held his hand down to her and lifted her to her feet. Harper snorted again but before she could reach out and pet her new friend, Henry wrapped his arms around her waist and kissed her lips fully. She knew she'd never tire of his kisses, because he could kiss like mad. She giggled when he pulled away.

"Why are you laughing at me?"

"I'm not laughing. I was just thinking you have mad kissing skills."

He laughed then and she joined him. The heavy tension of last night had lifted and it felt great.

Harper snorted again and she reached over and patted her jaw. Henry slowly raised his hand and patted Harper's jaw and she let him. The smile on his face was breathtaking.

"She's letting me touch her."

"It's beautiful."

"Hey there, Harper. Thank you for such a great gift this morning. But how did you manage to get out of your stall?"

"I was wondering that too."

Henry opened their stall door and held her hand until she stepped onto the concrete barn floor. Harper followed her to the stall. But she couldn't see anything different. She opened the door all the way and Harper walked right inside.

Everleigh shrugged. "I'll watch her today and see what she does."

"Okay. Mom and Dad brought a coffee pot and supplies. I'll get a pot going while you feed the horses."

"Perfect. Thank you."

She opened the feed bag, found the scoop Dr. Emily had pointed out last night, and began scooping the correct number of scoops into each feeding trough inside each stall. She smiled brightly at each horse as she fed them. "Good morning." She said to each one. Some nodded, a couple were still skittish, which she understood. They had time.

Once all the horses were fed, and she'd checked out Queenie's wounds, she joined Henry for a cup of coffee.

He was doing an inventory of the supplies and equipment so he could text his mom.

He found a wooden wire spool that he turned over and they used it as a table. He poured them each a coffee and pulled cheese and cookies from the cooler. As she nibbled, she heard a noise and looked down the barn to see Harper's head over the stall door. With her lips, she managed to play with the latch on her stall door.

She whispered. "Look."

He watched in silence for a few minutes then they both burst out laughing as Harper came trotting toward them.

"You're a Houdini." He chuckled.

He stood and Harper backed up. Her eyes rounded in fear.

Everleigh stood. "I'll bet that's why he beat her. She got out. She's afraid of you now."

He nodded and slowly lifted his hand with half of his cookie left. Harper stared at the cookie, then at Henry. Her eyes came to Everleigh's then back to the cookie. She took a step forward and waited. Then another. She snorted and bobbed her head, but Henry stood perfectly still. Finally, the cookie won, and Harper gently nibbled the cookie from Henry's hand.

He softly said, "I see you like cookies. Not sure how Lara will feel about me giving my cookies to horses, but I'll tell her it was a bonding tool."

He chuckled and so did she. She pet Harper on the neck. "Are you trying to steal my boyfriend?"

Harper nodded and snorted and both she and Henry laughed. What a beautiful morning. Her heart felt close to bursting.

An alarm on Henry's phone rang and he glanced at it. "I have to pick you up to head to the meeting in an hour."

"Oh, I almost forgot. Holy shit, we have to go."

"Secure the feed. Let's get Harper into her stall. I'll zip-tie her latch until we come back. As soon as your negotiations are over today, we'll come back here."

"Sounds good."

She managed to get Harper into her stall. Henry secured the latch. She checked the water troughs in each stall and they headed to the HOG to shower and get ready for the meeting. She was more eager than ever to get the negotiations worked out. And today she'd tell Casper that she was off duty for a while. Her stomach still twisted slightly thinking about it, but she easily set it aside when she thought of Harper's big brown eyes staring back at her. She had a new purpose in life and that was helping these horses and being Henry's girl. Which, made her her own girl. She was learning who Everleigh Hayes was. She liked the thought of that. She couldn't wait to tell her sister.

They hurried through the kitchen of the HOG and she jumped in the shower first while Henry gathered up some food for them. He showered after her and they companionably got ready together. A silent prayer went up that it would always be so cordial.

All the way to the town hall, she gathered her thoughts on today's meeting, the reminder of yesterday's with Craig seemed like light years ago.

They arrived with only a minute to spare. Gerard and Jasiah were the only two there from Hickory Hills and she hoped that was a good sign.

She sat across from them, but when she looked into Gerard's face, she gasped. He'd been beaten terribly. Both eyes were blackened. His lips were cut. His face was purple almost everywhere.

"Gerard, I am so sorry. Are you alright?"

"I'll be fine. The doctor in town here saw me early this morning. I don't have broken bones. I'm just beat up."

Henry's voice had a tinge of anger attached to it when he asked, "Did you find him?"

35

Henry stared at Gerard and remembered when Kenna had come down the mountain looking similar. Craig had to go. He'd never let peace fall on Glen Hollow or Hickory Hills.

Jasiah responded. "No. He's out there somewhere. We still have guys out there searching."

"Are they trustworthy?"

"I think they are."

The mayor entered the conference room and froze when he saw Gerard's face. Mayor Rayleigh Winters leaned forward. "Gerard. What in the hell happened to you?"

Gerard sucked in a deep breath. "Craig and I came to blows."

"I sure as hell hope he looks as bad as you do."

"I got a few punches in, but he got more. He sucker punched me before I knew what was happening."

"I'll be damned." Mayor Winters shook Everleigh's hand, then his.

Finally the president of the town council entered the
room. He reached out and shook hands with Mayor
Winters, Everleigh, and himself. He then turned to Gerard
and Jasiah. "I'm Zahn Krueger, president of the town
council."

Gerard leaned forward the best he could and held out
a bruised hand. Zahn gently took his hand and shook it,
then Jasiah's. "It looks as though you've had an accident,
Mr. Weston."

Gerard only nodded, Jasiah spoke. "Craig Howard
flipped out last night and created quite the shit show. He
damaged structures, items within reach, and sucker
punched my dad then continued to beat on him until he
was pulled off. Then he fled into the woods. We have men
out looking for him. They've been looking all night."

Heads shook around the table and Everleigh broke the
silence. "Mr. Weston, do..."

"Please call me Gerard."

"Thank you. Gerard, do you and Jasiah come with
authority to make a deal?"

"Yes. Ma'am. After Craig fled last night, the remaining
council agreed enough was enough. I was named president of the BRR until we formally disband."

"When will you disband?"

"When an agreement has been reached and we begin
seeing progress on utilities, we'll formally disband and
join the town of Glen Hollow."

"And this is unanimous?"

"Yes, ma'am."

Henry watched Everleigh address each man in the
room. You'd never know she was the only woman in the
room, and she sure didn't seem diminished by it. He'd
remember to tell her that tonight. Her job didn't give her

independence. The way she handles people gives her the independence she has. She's confident in herself. She's strong and smart and amazing. His opinion. But he was right.

Everleigh glanced his way then grinned. "As to the water. Henry took me to the other side of the mountain last night and showed me the field along Mr. Geoffrey Kurtz's farm. It appears the town water department could expand to that side of the mountain and build a water tower at the edge of Mr. Kurtz's farm. The water would be easier to bring up the mountain on that side due to less rock. The town currently has plans to expand sewer and water over there next summer anyway, so this would simply expand that plan. Water could be underway by February of this coming year. The project is slated to take four months. The construction of the water tower would only add another month to that timeline. Mr. Zahn, can you agree this is in the best interest of the town and the BRR to bring peace?"

Mr. Zahn shifted in his chair. His eyes glanced in Gerard's direction, and it was pretty hard in the face of what the situation was to say no. He nodded his head. "Yes. I do agree and I have the authority to enter into that agreement."

"Gerard, do you agree to this timeline?"

"I do agree."

"Mayor, how do you feel about this?"

"I fully agree."

Everleigh then typed in her laptop and addressed the electricity and the timeline. Next up was getting the townspeople to employ the citizens of Hickory Hills. That's when Henry stood.

"I'm finalizing and taking possession this afternoon of

the DeWitt farm. I'll need some strong hands to help me get the barn and fields in condition as soon as possible. I'll happily hire any Hickory Hills residents who want to work with me on my farm."

All heads turned in his direction and Jasiah nodded and smiled. "I'll find you the workers Mr. Delany."

He nodded toward Jasiah, but when he sat down, he smiled at Everleigh. She swallowed and nodded in his direction and his heart swelled. She was proud of him. He was fucking proud of her.

They waded through the treaty and the changes that needed to be made. They addressed the roads and how they'd need to be improved and widened so equipment could be brought up. Security was addressed.

Within three hours, an agreement was reached.

Everleigh smiled at each of them. "Thank you all for agreeing to terms in such a way as to move these negotiations forward quickly and smoothly. My last question for you Gerard and Jasiah is, what will you do when you find Craig?"

Jasiah responded. "We wanted to ask about that. If this agreement is official, can Dad make a complaint such that Craig can be arrested?"

Everleigh turned to the mayor. "I think that's your department. What do you think of that?"

The mayor stood. "Let me call the sheriff and check some of the laws. I'm not sure if the treaty would supersede any agreement. Technically, it happened before an agreement was reached, but after negotiations had begun. May I get back to you on this?"

"Absolutely." Everleigh addressed Gerard. "When you find him, he'll be angry. What will you do to keep him in line and not poison the well afterwards?"

"If the sheriff can't arrest him for this and put him in jail, we're building a jail of our own up there and we'll lock him up. A crime is a crime and between the beating of me and Ms. Lawrence before me and the damage he created last night, he's proven to be a danger to all. "

36

After shaking hands with them, she let out a heavy sigh as Henry escorted her to his truck. He opened the passenger door for her but before she could step in, he hugged her close and kissed her lips in that way he did. She loved it. "Congratulations Ev. You did an enormous job in a few short days, and you did it beautifully."

"Thank you. Craig helped though. He'd hate knowing that, but he did."

Henry chuckled and she enjoyed the sound. "You're right, he'd hate it. I hope we get the chance to tell him that."

She buckled herself in and they headed toward the HOG. "I thought we were headed to the horses."

"Well, today I thought we should dress for it. And I want to see what my mom found out and, I have to get the keys for the house. My parents did that for me today."

She laughed. "It's so exciting. All of it."

His laugh filled the truck and she closed her eyes and committed it to memory. It was the best sound.

"Uh-oh. You're about to meet them all."

"Who?"

He pointed to a couple of big trucks in the parking area of the HOG. Her car sat there, tires renewed, and people stood outside chatting with each other. Hawk and Roxanne were there also.

"These are the women of GHOST. My parents' generation. They're here to pick the carcass of my house." He turned to look at her. "Our house."

"Oh. Okay." She inhaled a deep breath. "Are you giving it all away?"

"No. I think we go in first and really look at what's in there. If you want to keep something, say so. They will take anything else. And, in a way, it's beautiful because, look..." He pointed to buckets and rags and cleaning supplies as well as mops and brooms standing at the back of one of the trucks. "They'll clean for us too!"

She laughed and he joined her. They high-fived.

Once they'd exited the truck, Henry took her hand and pulled her forward. "Hello, everyone. I'll hug you all in a minute. But, first, I'd like to introduce you to Everleigh Hayes, who just finished successfully negotiating a peace deal with the BRR and the town of Glen Hollow."

Cheering. Clapping. Congratulations filled her head. Henry then pulled her forward, hugged the first woman closest to them and introduced her to them. "Sophie Turner is Tate's mom." She was wrapped in a hug before she could get her hand out to shake. And, she was proud of herself for not totally stiffening up. "Bridget Dunbar is Aidyn's mom."

Another set of arms wrapped her tightly. "Jax Sager is Maya and Myles' mom." Jax hugged her then grinned. "We're huggers, girl. Get with us."

"I will. Thank you." Jax laughed and nudged their shoulders together. "It takes some getting used to."

"Isabella Masters is Addy's mom."

"It's nice to meet you."

Isabella wrapped her in a soft hug. "It's nice to meet you too."

Henry then clapped his hands to get attention. "Mom. What happened today?"

His mom stepped forward and hugged him. "I'm happy to hand you the keys to your new home." He took the keys, and his smile was beautiful. He held them up to her and winked. "And I'm in the middle of typing up your agreement with Case Evans on the purchase of seven horses, all the feed, the remaining hay in the barn and on the field. His hay baler, his plow, his disk, all the tack and supplies in his barn to go with the horses. The agreement will be signed later today."

He hugged his mom and spun her around. "Thanks for doing that. Did he give you trouble?"

"He blustered a bit. But I'm rather smart, and after about an hour of dealing with his shit, I called your dad in. You know his mad-mug look? That did it."

Henry's head flew back, and his laughter came straight up from his belly. He kissed his mom's cheek. He turned and grabbed her in both arms and spun her around. "Did you hear that? We have horses!"

"I did." She hugged him tightly and the women all began chatting away. When her feet hit the ground again, Henry then held her hand and addressed the women.

"Everleigh is staying. We're moving in together. She's going to rehab the horses. I'm working on the farm. I'm going to hire some folks from Hickory Hills to come down and help with the initial work since there's so much."

She was pulled and hugged all over again. The last hug though, was Roxanne who held her close and whispered in her ear. "I told you it would work out. Follow your heart."

"Thank you."

"Okay." Henry continued. "So, we have to change clothes. Mom has an agreement to draw up and then we have to go feed and water the horses before we can go to the house. Then, Everleigh and I will run through and pick and choose what items we want to keep, the rest will be up for grabs."

More cheers.

Two trucks with horse trailers pulled into the driveway and his dad and Tate jumped out. His dad shook his hand and hugged him.

"Congratulations, son. We thought we could move the horses over while you're busy doing everything else."

"That would be great, Dad." He glanced at her and then back to his dad. "You know they'll be a bit skittish because you're men."

"I figured that. But since you have to go and get them fed, we figured we'd go at that time and move them first, then feed them in their new home."

Henry shrugged. "I honestly don't know if the stalls are ready for them."

His dad chuckled and she realized how similar they sounded. "Tate, Spencer, Myles, and I were there all day fixing the stalls, tossing down new bedding and getting their troughs set up and ready."

"Oh god, Dad, that's just wonderful. Thank you so damned much."

He reached forward and hugged his dad. "We're so

proud of you Henry, and we all want to help you out. What you're doing for those horses is wonderful."

Tate nodded and hugged Henry. "We're all here for you." Tate glanced at her. "Both of you."

37

He tried to remember a time in his life when he'd been this overwhelmed. But he couldn't think of one. So many changes were happening at once. And, to see all the love and support from family and friends...well that was stunning. He'd do anything for any of them, but to know they felt the same, for some weird reason, never occurred to him.

He tied his work boots as Everleigh used the bathroom. Standing, he began tossing clothes into a duffel bag. He wasn't quite sure where they'd sleep tonight. The barn, or the house, or come back here. But he'd guess that Everleigh would want to sleep in the barn so the horses wouldn't be scared. It was only one more night, and it was exciting in so many ways. Last night they'd talked softly, listened to the nickering, and snorts of their rooming companions. It was new. So much new. In some ways he was ready for things to settle down. But not just yet.

The bathroom door opened and Everleigh stepped out looking fresh somehow. She wore jeans that fit her legs and ass perfectly. A cute cap-sleeve pink t-shirt. Her hair was swept up in a ponytail on top of her head. She looked absolutely adorable.

He stood and scooped her up in his arms. Then he kissed her lips. Softly. Sweetly. Fully.

"I love you, Everleigh."

She giggled against his lips. "I love you. And, for the record, I love hearing that."

He grinned. "Me too."

"Deal. I'll say it often."

He chuckled, then patted her butt. She looked damned good in those jeans.

"Okay, so I'm packing a bag for tonight. Not sure where we'll stay. What do you think?"

"I was wondering the same thing. I can toss some clothes into a bag."

Everleigh pulled undergarments from the drawer and put them neatly in her suitcase. She turned and cocked her head adorably. "Should I pack everything? Are we coming back here?"

"I figured for myself I'd pack a couple of days' worth, in case I get super dirty, which is likely. But, figured I'd then come back and pack. For you, you don't have as much here right now, so it's probably better if you just pack it all up now."

She grimaced, and his heart fell. "I didn't mean to make it sound like you don't have anything."

She huffed out a cute little breath, then said, "It's not a lie. I don't have much."

He grinned and kissed her nose. "Well, besides what you have here, we have seven horses and a bunch of farm stuff. Plus a big ole' house."

She shrugged. "Boy, what a difference a day makes."

He chuckled and zipped up his bag. "I'll let you pack while I go out and visit and make arrangements with everyone."

"Okay." Her smile was radiant, her demeanor happy. It excited him all over again.

He walked through the house, the kitchen empty of people, which was unusual. Where was Helissa today? He hadn't given it much thought earlier, but now, he wondered if she was sick.

He deposited his bag in the back of his truck then walked to the group of family, friends, and co-workers, who were like family to him.

Tate grinned. "Are you ready?"

He laughed. "Pretty fucking ready." Tate clapped him on the back and laughed with him. Henry then remembered to ask. "Where's Helissa?"

"She had some things to do today."

He shrugged. It wasn't his business to get involved in people's lives. Hell, he could barely keep up with his own these days.

Everleigh came out of the HOG rolling her suitcase behind her. Henry met her halfway and picked up her suitcase. "Do you want to drive your car over to the farm?"

"Sure."

He kissed her, set her suitcase in the back of his truck and nodded. He turned, "Okay, let's hit the road."

His dad nodded, "We'll meet you at the Evans' farm."

"Sounds good." He turned to Everleigh, who grinned, then began striding to her car. He stared for a minute, because, damn, she looked great in those jeans. He turned and hopped in his truck as the others were loading themselves into vehicles.

The ride to the farm was short. Less than two miles as

he clocked it now. That would make it easy when he needed to join his team for work assignments. Which reminded him...He tapped his phone and scrolled to find Spencer's name.

"Miss me already?"

Henry laughed. "Yes. Can you tuck me in tonight?"

Spencer laughed on the other end of the phone. "Of course, baby. Should I sing you a lullaby too?"

Henry continued chuckling. "Hey, I'd like some security set up on the farm. Can you work on that with me?"

"Of course. When we get there, let's walk around and you can show me where you want cameras set up."

"Perfect. Thanks, Spence."

Things ran through his mind faster than he could gather them right now. Thank goodness he had great support. How many times had he thought that, just today?

He stopped in front of the house. Everleigh pulled her car in alongside his truck and he grinned at her out the window. Her smile lit the sky. It made his heart race. From the outside watching, it likely looked like he'd never had a girlfriend before.

Jumping from his vehicle, he pulled his duffel and Everleigh's suitcase from the back and clumped up the steps to the porch. Everleigh stood next to him.

Glancing down at her, his lips turned up into a smile, "Ready?"

"Ready."

He turned the key in the lock, for the first time as a homeowner. Surreal.

Waiting for Everleigh to walk in first, he followed with their luggage.

"So, first things first, we'll need a way to mark what furniture is staying. The rest is up for grabs to the others."

Everleigh turned her head and stared up into his eyes. Her pretty lips turned down into a slight frown. "I'm afraid I'm not going to be good at this. I don't know a thing about design. Furniture. Pictures. None of it."

38

She hated feeling inadequate. Her parents expected perfection from her and her sister and here she was, her first day as a girlfriend and she was failing.

The hard knot that formed in her throat threatened to suffocate her. She stared into Henry's eyes, waiting for the disapproval. That sickening look that her father gave her when she was less than perfect. His brows bunched together and that hateful pinch of skin between his brows that always seemed to stick out when he was angry.

Instead, Henry leaned down and kissed her forehead. "Should I ask my mom to come in and help out? After all, she and Sophie designed the HOG."

Relief flooded her body, and she allowed her shoulders to relax. "That would be awesome."

He chuckled. "We've got this Ev. Even if we don't do all the work for our place, we have a support system beyond all support systems."

She swallowed the emotion that raced up her throat. Blinking furiously so her tears didn't spill down her cheeks and nodded. "I've always had to rely on myself. It'll take me a minute to get used to this."

"You take the time you need. I'll be right here with you."

He kissed her forehead once again then turned toward the door and called out to his mom. "Mom, can you come in a minute?"

"Sure."

Henry stepped back and held the door for his mom. The second she stepped inside her eyes darted between her and Henry.

Henry took the lead, which she was grateful for. The last thing she wanted to do was break down in Roxanne's arms two days in a row.

"So, neither Everleigh nor I have any design savvy. We were hoping you'd take the lead on this place."

"Really? Oh, you have no idea the visions that have been running through my head these past few days. I'd love to."

Roxanne stepped toward her. "Are you sure Everleigh?"

Her head bobbed. "I'm certain. I don't know the first thing about designing a house."

"If at any time this gets to be too much, just let me know."

"I will. Then, I'll go out by the horses and let you do your thing. What you did at the HOG is amazing."

"Okay. Then, let's get the others in here and we'll get started. If you two want to go to the Evans' place and work with the horses, we'll get to cleaning and arranging and organizing in here. I bought a bunch of things to get you started and it turns out, so did the others."

Her eyes rounded. "Oh my god, I certainly didn't mean you had to do all the work here. There's a lot."

Roxanne laughed. "You see all those people out there? I'm not doing all the work. I'm directing. There's a difference."

Henry laughed. "Trust me. It's better if we get out of the way. We can change anything you don't like."

"I can't imagine I won't like anything. I mean, I just can't imagine it."

Roxanne kissed her forehead. "Go on and help your horses. By bedtime tonight you'll have a bedroom, a kitchen, and at least a living room. Maybe more if we can manage it."

A clattering sounded from the kitchen and both she and Henry looked at each other. He began striding to the kitchen and she followed.

There was a woman in the kitchen cleaning.

"Helissa, I wondered where you were today."

"Your mama asked me to shop and prepare some meals for the two of you and to have a dinner planned for the crew this evening. But I had to clean the kitchen first. I'm almost ready to start cooking."

Henry began laughing and turned to his mom. "Anything else you've had in the works today?"

She shrugged. "I take care of my children. You go and do things you're good at, I'll take care of this."

Roxanne winked at her and all she could do was grin. It did relieve a ton of pressure about cooking and keeping a house. All things she was going to need to do.

Henry took her hand, and they walked through the dining room to the front door. Outside, the ladies were carrying in the buckets and cleaning supplies and mops and brooms and the sight was something she'd never witnessed before.

Once they'd situated themselves in Henry's truck, he started pulling out of the driveway but took her hand. "At any time you feel blown away with any of this, we can call it a day."

She chuckled. "Thank you. I was overwhelmed when we pulled into the HOG earlier."

He laughed. "Me too. It's been...surreal."

She nodded but smiled at him. At least they were over-whelmed together. Not that it was good that they were both overwhelmed, but good that they were in this together. At least there was that.

At the Evans' farm she heard the horses whinnying and it sounded like they were stressed. She jogged toward the barn to see Tate and Hawk trying to subdue Harper. She ambled toward them and softly called out to Harper.

"Hey, Harper, it's all right. We're taking you to your new home with Henry and me. We're going to take care of you. All of you."

She slowly stepped closer, and Harper bobbed her head. Holding her hand out to Harper, it took a few minutes for the horse to calm.

Once Harper had calmed enough to have her bridle put on, Everleigh slowly fastened it on. She opened the stall door, and calmly walked with Harper to the first trailer. Harper balked slightly at the trailer, but she'd been prepared for this and braced herself until Harper was ready.

Slowly entering the trailer, she dropped the bridle and eased herself out the man-door on the side. Hawk chuck-led. "How did you learn to do that?"

"In the Army they have programs that kids of the

service members can enroll in. I enrolled in learning about horses. Every year it was a different course, but I learned a ton during my time there."

"That's fantastic, Everleigh."

Her cheeks heated at the praise from Henry's father. Praise hadn't come that easy from her parents. She'd need to let all that baggage go. Her parents were good people, they just weren't great parents. Not everyone was.

39

It took them four hours to move the seven horses to their farm and set them up in their stalls. The fact that the guys had done the bulk of the work during the day helped tremendously.

He was tired, sweaty, and hungry. Mostly hungry. Maybe tired. Ack, it was hard to tell what he mostly was. But, hanging the last of the saddles, bridles, and other articles in the tack room, he was ready for something to eat.

He stepped onto the middle apron in the barn and saw Everleigh talking to Harper. "This is your new home. I hope you'll be happy here."

He grinned as he watched her talk to the horse. For her part, Harper nodded and snorted as if she understood. Everleigh was a horse whisperer.

She turned her head and smiled the brightest smile he'd ever seen. "Harper and I are in agreement that it's quite nice here."

He chuckled. "I'm happy to hear that. I think it is too."

He bent down and kissed her lips. She pulled back. "I think I stink."

He laughed from deep down in his belly. "You can't smell more than I do." He turned and saw his dad and Tate moving something outside. "Or any of us for that matter."

She giggled.

"Let's go eat." He held his hand out to her and the instant they connected, his heart sang. Stepping outside, he saw Spencer up on a ladder on the side of the barn.

"Hey, Spence. Let's eat."

"Yep. I'll be right there."

They gathered folks as they neared the house and that's when his stomach growled in earnest. The aromas coming from inside made him feel like a starving man nearing a feast.

Inside they froze. The transformation was astounding. "Holy shit." He whispered.

"Yeah." Everleigh responded.

His mom entered from the dining room. "What do you think?"

The living room, which was directly across the foyer from the front door had been rearranged, cleaned, and furniture from other rooms had been moved in. It was cozy and it looked like it could be in a magazine.

"Now, keep in mind the wallpaper is old and it should be removed or replaced. I'm happy to work with you on that. But, for purposes of getting you settled in, this is what we've come up with."

He and Everleigh stood speechless for a few moments. She finally found her voice first.

"I never would have come up with that arrangement. It looks like a scene from a movie."

His mom beamed. "I think it turned out lovely. Once we have the floors refinished and the painting complete, it'll be simply stunning. The wood in this house is amazingly preserved."

He moved gently into the living room and turned around slowly to take in all that had been done in such a short time. He turned as he took in the fireplace with its gleaming wood and ornate marble façade. He hadn't noticed the intricate carving in the wood mantel before. It hadn't been his focus at all actually. The hearth matched the marble around the fireplace, and it shined.

"Bridget scrubbed on this fireplace for an hour. It was so dirty and dusty you couldn't see what was beneath."

"She did an amazing job." He breathed.

Across the room from the fireplace was a wall of bookshelves. There were a few encyclopedias on the shelves, and miscellaneous books scattered here and there, but for the most part, the shelves were clean, but empty.

His eyes scanned the detailing on the shelves, it matched the fireplace. He'd enjoy this room. It felt homey and comfortable. The rug that covered the floor was worn and the edges frayed, but that was replaceable.

He turned to see Everleigh transfixed on the detailing. "What do you think, Ev?"

"I don't have words."

He swallowed the lump in his throat.

She stepped to him and wrapped an arm around his waist. "It looks completely different."

The windows were clean and the light that filtered in made everything sparkle.

"It does."

His mom chuckled. "There's more."

With Everleigh's hand in his, his mom led them up the

staircase to the second level. The stairs had been wiped down and the wood gleamed as they ascended them. At the top landing, his mom turned left and led them to the master bedroom.

She stepped inside and smiled brightly. Sophie was just finishing up dusting the windowsill across the room. She turned and grinned as they stepped inside.

His mom nodded. "Sophie and I found pieces of furniture in other rooms and mixed and matched until we liked these together."

Sophie laughed. "Don't ask how many times we've moved things around."

Everleigh chuckled but was otherwise as speechless as he was. It was stunning. The ornate headboard was an antique white which had been sanded at one time to show the wood through.

"We found the headboard in another room. It was attached to the wall, but we thought it worked better in here. That room, however, will need to wait to have its day."

Everleigh touched the comforter on the bed, her brows furrowed together. "This is new."

"It is." His mom chuckled. "Some things need to be new. Bedding is a thing for me. So, this is all courtesy of Sophie and Gaige."

He turned and saw Sophie's smile, and he instantly went to her and wrapped her in a hug. "Thank you, Sophie. For everything. I can't tell you how much I appreciate it."

She squeezed him back. "The look on your face is payment enough. I'm happy to help out."

Everleigh swallowed. "Thank you, Sophie. This is amazing."

The comforter was a deep blue with a slight sheen to it. The contrast to the headboard was remarkable.

The dresser gleamed. The dark wood stood against the far wall from the bed and on either side of the bed were small round tables with delicate lamps perched on top.

He scraped his hand through his hair. "I'm simply overwhelmed."

His mom and Sophie laughed and high-fived each other. "It's not often we make our children speechless."

"Yeah." Was all he could say.

40

They continued their tour of the house. Not all of the rooms had been cleaned, but the women promised to be here for the weekend to clean and get them set up for success here.

The kitchen had been scrubbed and currently Isabella and Yvette were scrubbing the cupboards as Helissa cooked. The aromas wafted around the house, and she smelled a clean environment and fresh baked bread. Her mouth watered. She couldn't remember the last time she had fresh bread straight from the oven.

Henry swallowed as he looked at everything that had been done. The women chatted and giggled, and the home felt just like that. A home. People were happy here, and she hoped that would continue. Henry spoke to his friends and she stepped closer to Helissa. "Thank you for all you've done today."

"You are welcome. I'm happy to help out."

Everleigh nodded. "Would you be willing to teach me how to cook?"

"Really? I would love that. I can come here one day a week and we'll make meals. Is that good for you?"

"It's good." Her bottom lip began to quiver, and her eyes filled with tears. How could there be so many good people in one small place?

"You don't cry. It's all good. I'm from here. People help each other. I'll help you. One day, you'll help me. That's it."

She nodded and Helissa handed her a napkin. She dabbed at her eyes and inhaled a deep breath. Holy crap what a whirlwind week. Holy crap!

Helissa clapped her hands. "Dinner is ready. Please let the men know."

Sophie had just entered the kitchen. "I'll run out." She turned and exited the room.

There were plates set up on the counter and silverware. "Where did all this come from?" She asked anyone who would answer.

Roxanne, who always was the picture of poise and grace smiled at her. "This was all here. Mr. DeWitt left it. When we found the cupboards filled with items, we called Zander and he called Mr. DeWitt who said, and I quote. 'Tell them it's on me. Those dishes are antiques. They can keep them or sell them. Whatever.'"

"Wow. That's amazing." She picked up a plate and looked at the pattern. They were white with different patterns on the separate sizes of plates. Isabella neared. "I believe these are Wedgwood Plates. They are wonderful plates, and it appears the entire set is here. Twelve of each plate, bowl, coffee cup, saucer, and the serving dishes too. Not a bad way to start out."

"That's unbelievable." She glanced up to see Henry watching her, his disbelief as evident as hers likely was. He winked at her and butterflies took off in her stomach.

Lately they'd had precious little time to just be. She looked forward to that. Just being. Hopefully, he wouldn't grow bored with her.

The noise level rose as the men entered the house. Hawk was first. "We need to wash up. Which bathroom should we use?"

Roxanne looked her way, but she had no idea. She shrugged and Roxanne smiled sweetly. "The bathroom just off the linen closet near the dining room has been cleaned."

They had a linen closet? She hadn't seen that. She was going to need some time to wander around this place and find everything. Which made her wonder where her suitcase had gone. Likely in the master bedroom upstairs, but she didn't remember seeing a closet up there. She'd walk around later.

The men came back in one at a time and picked up a plate and began filling them with fried chicken, roast beef, mashed potatoes, gravy, green beans, and fresh bread. The bread still steamed as it laid on the plate, the butter would melt right into it. Her tummy growled.

Hawk turned as he dumped a giant spoonful of mashed potatoes on his plate. "I'm sorry. You and Henry should go first."

"No, please, as our guests, go ahead. It's the least we can do for all you've done for us."

Her eyes darted to Roxanne who winked at her, and she took that as approval. Though she wasn't sure what she was seeking approval for. Just because they were Henry's parents, she did want them to like her. And, she wanted their approval. She'd seldom had her parents' approval.

Taking a deep breath, she leaned back against the

counter and told herself to let it go. It was time. Let the past go. She had her sister. She had Henry and she had all these amazing people in her life. That was more than so many other people ever had in theirs.

"Are you alright?" His deep voice wrapped around her and goosebumps formed on her arms. Yes, she liked his voice. A lot.

"I am. How about you?"

He chuckled. "I'm doing about as good as you." He leaned down near her ear. "I didn't know we had a linen closet."

She burst out laughing. "I didn't either and was just thinking we'd need to go through each room and figure it all out. Like, where are our clothes?"

His brows bunched together. "Yeah, where did they go?"

"See? We have some exploring to do."

He bent down and kissed her temple and she closed her eyes. His arm slid around her shoulders and she leaned into him as she watched their guests, their very first guests, fill their plates, laugh, joke around, eat and enjoy each other. The large dining room table filled as they took their food in and sat. It was lovely. Like a family. It made her heart fill with so much emotion, she was afraid she'd blabber on like a baby if she let herself think about it too long. So, she didn't.

They were the last to fill their plates and Henry squeezed her shoulders. "Our turn."

She looked up at him and smiled. "You first, please."

"I'm not even going to argue. I'm starving and wait until you taste Helissa's fried chicken."

"Shit, I've been mooning over the bread since I first walked in here."

He chuckled. "Okay. Let's do it."

They filled their plates and found the dining room full, so the two of them stepped out onto the porch and sat in their rocking chairs.

The horses had been turned out to pasture, all except Queenie. She had to stay in until her wounds were healed. But the others were outside looking simply picture perfect. They grazed in the long grass. Their tails swished back and forth, and they looked peaceful.

"This is perfect out here."

Henry's mouth was full of food so he simply nodded. Once he'd swallowed his food he said, "You were right about this."

The door opened and Roxanne stepped out. "We're sorry to make you come out here."

Henry laughed. "Don't be. Look at our view."

Roxanne looked out into the pasture and stared for a moment. She eventually sat on the top step and watched the horses just as they were doing. "Wow, this is wonderful, Henry."

He grinned. "I know. It's perfect."

Roxanne glanced at her. "Do you like it, Everleigh?"

"I do. Absolutely."

41

Henry watched Everleigh as she took care of Queenie's wounds. He, for his part, checked each stall door to ensure they were all closed. He grinned at Harper. "Sorry for the extra lock Harper, but your escape skills have to be tamed."

Harper bobbed her head and snorted in disapproval. He chuckled and moved on. He checked the tack room once again, enjoying the way it looked with the harnesses and bridles neatly lined up on the wooden pegs.

"You did a great job in here." Everleigh praised.

"Thanks. I like how it turned out."

Everleigh turned and looked down the length of the barn and he did the same. "It's surreal."

She shook her head. "That's an understatement."

They chuckled, stared in awe and, at least for his part, enjoyed this moment. It was finally quiet.

"Are we sleeping in the house or out here tonight?"

Her head tilted up, her eyes stared into his. "Do you mind if we sleep in the house? I'm simply exhausted and these ladies make a fair amount of noise."

He laughed. "No, I don't mind and yes they do."

"I think they seem settled enough. They've had a busy day too."

"Dr. Zsidai will stop out in the morning to check them all over. I think she'll be happy."

"I do too. I'm excited to see her reaction."

He chuckled, turned, and took Everleigh's hand in his. "Good night, ladies. Sleep tight."

Everleigh giggled and a couple of the horses snorted. He turned off the light in the tack room. Everleigh stepped out the man door of the barn, and he followed her, locking it up after them. They strolled hand in hand toward the house, and though there was still work to do, he was excited about the progress made today. By the end of the weekend, which was four more days, it would be unrecognizable. But, in a good way.

They entered the house, the aromas from today's food still lingered in the air. "Smells good in here." He absently stated.

"It does."

Everleigh sighed. "I'm going to go up and take a shower, if that's alright."

"Of course, it is. This is your house too."

She shrugged slightly and he knew it would take some time for her to feel comfortable here. Part of him worried she'd grow bored in a few months. She was used to picking up and going somewhere new after each job. Her job here was nearly settled and he wondered how she'd handle not packing up and moving again.

The water in the shower turned on and he wandered to the kitchen and pulled a beer from the refrigerator. He'd join her in the shower, but he was dog-ass tired. She was too. They'd worked their tails off today.

He received a text and chuckled when he saw Spencer's name.

"Sorry I didn't finish the security system. I'll have it finished before the weekend is over. I had to order a few things."

He quickly responded. "No worries. I don't anticipate any trouble. Craig's still out there, but if he comes here he's a dead man. He must know that."

The ellipsis bounced as Spencer typed. "I can't imagine he'd think otherwise."

Henry sat back in the rocking chair and stared out at his farm. Life was exciting right now.

The screen door behind him opened and Everleigh's soft footsteps across the porch floor neared him. He turned to see her freshly showered body, encased in workout shorts and a tank top. "You look gorgeous and revived."

She giggled. "I certainly feel revived. The shower felt heavenly."

"Then I'm jumping in."

He kissed her lips as he stepped passed her, then headed to the refrigerator and pulled a seltzer from inside for her. He stepped out on the porch as she sat in her rocking chair and handed her the seltzer. "Here you go. I'll be out soon."

"Thank you."

He entered the house, still amazed at all that had transpired here today. His eyes landed on a narrow door near the entrance to the dining room. He ambled over and opened it up. Linen closet.

Grinning, he trudged up the stairs, eager to wash off today's sweat and grime.

His phone chimed once, alerting him to a text and he

saw his mom's name on his phone. "I love you."

He shook his head. She was something, his mom. "I love you too. Thank you again for everything."

He sent his text, then started the shower to warm, went to the master bedroom and searched for a closet. He found the closet and there sat his duffle bag. Everleigh had hung her clothes to one side of the closet. He grinned. She was neat about it too.

Tossing his duffle on the bed, he began pulling his clean clothes from inside. Opening the top drawer, he saw Everleigh had laid her undergarments to the left, leaving him plenty of room. He chuckled, added his undergarments to the drawer, minus one pair of clean underwear, and headed to the shower.

The instant the warm water flowed over his body, he began to feel better. There was something about a shower that could revive even the tiredest soul. He began mentally noting the things he wanted to accomplish tomorrow. First, he'd like to hire the men from Hickory Hills and get them working on the fences around the property. There would come a day he'd like to have cattle along with horses.

He'd need to ask the mayor how he contacted the BRR. They didn't have phones. He could take a drive up there, and maybe he'd do that tomorrow. While Craig was away, it'd be good to see how they operated up there.

He stepped from the shower and the bedroom light was on. The smile grew on his face as he neared the bedroom because he hoped he'd find Everleigh inside.

She did not disappoint.

The bed was large, clearly not from years gone by,

which was good. Everleigh was in the middle of the bed, a sheet pulled up over her breasts. She laid on her side, her head in her hand and a smile on her face. An hour ago he'd have said nothing could have made today better. Now, though, he knew that wouldn't have been true.

42

The smile on his face was what she'd hoped for. He had the best smile anyway, but right now, fresh from the shower, still a bit damp, his lips parted perfectly in a combination surprise and seduction, she grinned as he stalked toward her. The towel wrapped around his waist fell as he neared, and just how happy he was to see her was evident.

His knee perched on the bed, to allow his body to hover over hers easily. She fell to her back and stared up at the handsomest man she'd ever had the pleasure to meet. And right now, he was all hers. Her fingers slid up his arms, until she found his shoulders. Her hands continued to roam over his firm body as his lips devoured hers.

Their tongues danced beautifully together. His lips then kissed her jaw and to her neck. He sucked her skin into his mouth and she'd likely have a mark tomorrow, but it would be worth it. She'd never had a hickey before, and she liked these firsts she had with Henry.

His mouth and teeth grazed over her shoulder, then

down to cover her breast. He sucked her nipple into his mouth and feasted on it like a starving man enjoyed a meal. Her nipples pebbled tightly, which made them more sensitive to his touch. He kissed across her chest to the other nipple, and she moaned.

His fingers found her clit, and he wasted no time bringing her close to orgasm, only to pull his fingers away. Disappointment was soon forgotten, because he kissed his way down her belly, until his lips found her clit. He suckled her as her fingers dug into his still damp hair. When his thick fingers slid into her, she heard herself moan, but couldn't believe it had come from her. His finger slid in and out of her, the sounds of her wetness combined with the feeling of his mouth and fingers brought her to orgasm in a heartbeat. She felt the fire build, and she gasped his name as she fell over the edge.

He kissed his way up her body, but she was still reeling from her orgasm. He slid his cock into her, slowly. So very slowly. She could feel every inch as his deep throaty voice whispered. "I love you, Everleigh."

She lifted her legs to wrap around his ass, and she met him thrust for thrust. She wanted to show him how he made her feel. Her body heated, but so did his. His arm slid beneath her back, and in one fluid motion, he'd flipped them over so she was on top of him. His hands instantly covered her breasts as she rode him.

Their eyes locked as she enjoyed how he felt inside of her. Her hands pushed against his firm chest as she lifted herself up and dropped down once again.

His eyes bored into hers. "Now."

She increased her speed, not sure how much energy she had. But she'd give this man pleasure, no matter what she had to do.

His hands planted on her hips and he helped her up and down on his cock, until his body stiffened and his hands squeezed her hips tightly. He pushed her firmly down on his cock as he growled, and her second orgasm took her breath away.

She fell onto his chest and his arms wrapped her in his cocoon. There was no place on earth she'd rather be. Not now. Not ever.

His breathing was heavy near her ear, their bodies sweaty where they were joined but she didn't care in the least.

She woke a while later. Still on top of Henry. His breathing was even and steady and she enjoyed the calmness as they lay mingled together.

His arms tightened around her and he whispered in her ear. "Just a while longer."

She relaxed again against him. He squeezed her once more.

A few moments later, his arms relaxed and she slid off his body and laid on her back staring at the ceiling. The moonlight filtered beautifully through the trees and made the ceiling look as though the trees were dancing inside. She watched it for a few moments until her eyelids grew heavy and Henry's deep breathing lulled her back to sleep.

She woke to sunlight and the aroma of coffee. She used the bathroom, dressed quickly and padded downstairs to see Henry in the kitchen staring out the window.

"Good morning."

He turned, his face a work of art, his body big and brawny and oh-so-yummy. "Good morning."

He stepped into her arms and held her close. "Have you been up for a while?"

"Long enough to make coffee and enjoy the quiet. I think it'll be another busy day."

"Yeah. I think so too."

He kissed her forehead, then her lips, and poured her a cup of coffee. "Thank you."

She sat at the little wooden kitchen table and sipped her coffee. Henry sat across from her and stared into her eyes.

"What?" She giggled.

"I'm happy. Are you happy?"

"Yes. I'm happy. Why would you ask?"

"Just checking. I don't want to lose sight of the fact that this is all very new to you. Me too, but very new for you. If I seem to let go of that fact, will you remind me? Tell me if you're struggling."

Setting her cup on her saucer, she reached for his hand across the table. "I will tell you if I'm struggling. Will you tell me if you are?"

His smile was gorgeous. "I'll tell you."

"Deal."

He glanced at his watch, "Dr. Emily will be here in a half hour or so. Let's see what we can rustle up to eat."

She stood, leaned over and kissed him on the lips. "Let me help so I can learn."

He chuckled. "Okay. I'm not that great in the kitchen either, so we'll learn together."

43

Henry drove up the mountain and saw Gerard sitting near the fire pit in the middle of their compound. His back was slightly hunched over, and he was speaking with a woman. Both their heads turned as he neared.

"I've never come all the way up without being stopped on the road, or fear of being stopped on the road."

Gerard nodded. "That's the way it is now. Among many other changes here. Henry Delany, meet my sister, Hanalore Howard. Hana, this is Henry."

He reached forward and shook Hana's hand. She also had bruises on her face, not as bad as Gerard, but she'd been hit. It took him a moment, but Hanalore was also Craig's wife.

"How are you doing, Gerard?"

"I'm healing. So is Hana."

Henry shook his head. It was disgraceful to hit a woman. It boggled his mind how Craig had gotten this far.

"I'm sorry for your injuries. Have you found him yet?"

"No. We still have men out looking though."

"I hope they find him soon. We all need the peace of mind."

"That we do. What can I help you with?"

"I came up to see if there are four or five men who'd like to work for me on my farm. I have a fair amount of work to do, and I'll take anyone willing to do it."

Hana stepped back. "I'll go find Jasiah, he'll know who's looking for work."

"Thank you." He nodded to Hana and when she smiled he saw how similar she and Gerard looked. At least when they weren't beaten and bruised.

Gerard motioned to the bench alongside him. "Please take a seat and make yourself comfortable. It won't take long. I think there's quite a few men who'd be willing to go down the mountain and work."

"Good to hear." He sat on the wooden bench and stared into the ashes of the fire that had likely burned last night. The smell of fresh burnt wood and something else wafted in the air.

He turned his head to stare at Gerard, the man seemed sad and sore. "How are you really, Gerard?"

"I'm worried. Craig knows these mountains like the back of his hand. He can live on the land, he can hunt, and he can stalk us for days and days. I keep thinking if I sit out here, it'll bait him into coming out to finish me off. Then, hopefully, Jasiah or someone else will be able to finish him off." Gerard looked him in the eyes. "I know that sounds bad, I just don't know how any of us will be safe while he's around."

"I've worried and wondered the same thing. He's proven he will not abide by the laws of the town. He's fought any change from the beginning. And, he'll continue to poison the well, so to speak, as long as he's alive. Unless we can get him in a prison."

Gerard's head slowly shook. "No. He has to die. It's the only way."

"Well, we can't plan a murder and not go to jail ourselves. It's against the law."

Gerard's head slumped down further. "I'm aware."

Henry turned his body so he faced Gerard. "Don't do anything that will put you in prison for Craig. He isn't worth spending the rest of your life behind bars."

Gerard's sad eyes looked into his and he felt so damned sorry for this man. He was beaten and he seemed broken. His faded blue eyes, the left one with broken blood vessels, stared for a long time into his eyes. "I won't do anything...what do you call it? Premeditated."

He reached out and put his hand gently on Gerard's forearm. "I'm here, and so is my team if you need anything."

"Okay."

Footsteps came close and he sat up and watched as Jasiah and four men approached. "Good morning, Henry. This is Liam Price, Carson, Waylon, and Duffy Park. They're brothers. This is Henry Delany. He has work on a farm for you to do."

Henry stood and shook all of their hands. "I can bring you down and back home tonight if you like. I'm not sure if you have a vehicle to use."

Liam was the first to respond. "We have the old truck. We can follow you down."

"Sounds good." He shook Gerard's hand and whispered. "Don't do anything stupid. He's not worth it."

"I won't." Gerard stood and looked at the men going down the mountain. "Make us proud."

Liam nodded and grinned. "We'll work our asses off."

The others grinned but said nothing. It was a test for all of them. It was a new beginning. Henry turned to the men. "I'll pay you fifteen dollars an hour. I'm in need of fences to be built. I'll work along with you, at least for the first half of the day. We'll feed you lunch and dinner before you come back up. Are these arrangements agreeable to you?"

They looked at him in surprise and amazement. Carson finally said, "You'll feed us too?"

"Yes. We're feeding everyone at the house. The place is crawling with people these days. We've got a whole crew in and out of the house getting things pulled together."

"Wow. That's agreeable to me." Carson responded.

Waylon chuckled. "Carson eats like a horse, you'll likely change your mind tomorrow."

Henry laughed. "We'll see."

He strode to his truck feeling like this could work out nicely. In a short time he was going to have his farm up and running. They already had seven horses. And he had Everleigh. There wasn't much more he could ask for really.

44

Everleigh finished her email to Casper. Her heart hammered in her chest, but before she could lose her nerve, she hit send. She inhaled a deep breath and closed the lid on her laptop.

She carried her laptop upstairs and laid it on the dresser, made the bed, then headed down to feed and water the horses.

Just as she stepped off the porch, Dr. Emily's truck pulled into the driveway. She waved and jogged to the barn.

"Good morning."

"Good morning. How did your first night go?"

"I think it went great. I'm just now going in to say good morning to the ladies."

Dr. Emily laughed. "I'll be right in."

Everleigh opened the big barn door and said, "Good morning, ladies."

Harper's head poked over the stall door first. She snorted and Everleigh rubbed her satiny nose. Lady, Diamond, Miss Penny Mae were next and she greeted each one with a smile and a rub on the nose. Across the aisle, she greeted Jazzy, Sugar, and Queenie. Dr. Emily entered the barn and chuckled.

"What a different life these girls have now. It's beautiful to see."

Everleigh turned to her and smiled. "Thank you."

Dr. Emily set her big case on the ground. "I'll start with Queenie. Any issues with her wounds?"

"No, she lets me doctor her. She's gentle. It's almost like she knows we're trying to help her."

"She does. She's been injured before. Queenie was Cash's wife's horse. He took a big dislike to her because his wife left her behind. Poor girl had no say in any of it."

Everleigh's stomach hurt hearing this. Poor girl went through so much just because of who owned her. Nothing she'd done wrong. People sucked sometimes.

"Well, I can guarantee, she will never deal with beatings or misery ever again. It's our mission to rehab horses who have been abused."

"How did you get involved with horses?"

"It was my escape as a kid. My family is a military family, and we moved a lot. But there was usually a program for the kids at each base to teach us about horses. I reveled in it."

"That's wonderful. Have you thought about bringing school kids out here and teaching them about horses?"

Everleigh stared at Dr. Emily for a moment. "I hadn't thought about that. It's something I can talk to Henry about though."

"Okay. Well, I better get started. Any other concerns while I'm here?"

Everleigh cocked her head and looked at Harper, who stared out the stall door at her. "No. Just make sure their general health is good. We're hoping we'll be able to breed these gals one day."

"There's no reason you couldn't breed any of them. They're generally healthy for that. It's the mental issues of fear from being hit and the unpredictability of their former life that may get in the way. Queenie is the exception. She'll likely be the hardest to bring around."

"I'll keep trying though. Until we're fast friends."

Dr. Emily chuckled and set out to tend to Queenie's wounds while Everleigh began feeding and watering.

Spencer stepped into the barn. "Morning."

Everleigh grinned. "Good morning. Dr. Emily, this is Spencer Lawson. A co-worker of Henry's."

"Good morning, Spencer."

"Morning."

"Everleigh, I'll be setting up cameras in here today. Will the horses be out to pasture at some point?"

"In about an hour. I need to feed and water them first. Will that work?"

"Yes, ma'am."

He left barn and then came back in with a large spool of wire. He started bringing in other equipment. Then he brought in a long antenna. Harper began snorting, bobbing her head and stomping at the ground. Everleigh moved to the stall to see what was inside. Dr. Emily did the same thing. Harper's movements became more pronounced, and she reared up and kicked the stall.

Everleigh turned to the doctor, her brows furrowed and bunched together. "What's wrong with her?"

Dr. Emily shook her head. "I don't know."

Everleigh stepped aside then turned to see Spencer waving the antenna around as he wrapped the end of it with tape.

"Spencer. It's you."

"What?" His confused face turned to her.

"She thinks that's a switch."

His eyes rounded and he marched himself out of the barn. As soon as he was out of sight, Harper calmed.

Everleigh petted Harper's neck. "It's okay girl. I didn't think of that. But Spencer won't hurt you. Not ever."

As soon as she'd calmed completely, Everleigh went out to find Spencer. He stood alongside the barn, his shoulders drooped. "I'm sorry Everleigh, I never would hurt a horse."

"I know. You know. She doesn't understand."

He scraped his hand through his hair, his jaw clenched tightly.

"Hey, it's okay. It's a reminder to me that anything that looks like a switch, will need to be kept from them until we can reintroduce such things in a positive way. Simple as that."

"Okay. Shit. That makes me feel like shit."

"Don't worry on it. Like I said, it's a good reminder and we were here to calm her, so it's all going to be just fine."

Spencer nodded and took a deep breath. "I'll work out here until the horses are out of the barn."

"One of them, Queenie, will need to stay inside, but I can walk her while you're inside so she can stretch her legs. Give me a bit of time."

"I've got things I can do out here in the meantime."

"Awesome."

She entered the barn and found Dr. Emily back working on Queenie. Harper had calmed. All was right in the barn once again. She went to the feed room, filled a wheelbarrow with feed and began her chores. It was her first day actually doing full-fledged chores. And her heart had never been happier. She had a home, though she didn't know where most things were. And, she didn't know how to cook. But she'd learn. She had a purpose with the horses. And she'd find a way to make money with them. And, she had Henry. A man who had only lived in her dreams. Now she lived in his house.

45

The day had passed in what seemed like the blink of an eye. He'd barely seen Everleigh today, but he was looking forward to finding out how her day went. He'd worked with the Hickory Hills men and they were all hard workers. They learned what he wanted quickly and they were efficient. As soon as he could, he'd tell other farmers about their work ethic. They were used to working sunup to sundown, so to break for meals was a real kick to them. They came back to the field with full bellies and eager to work again.

He heard them ribbing each other and he chuckled. It sounded a lot like him and his friends. And why wouldn't it? They'd let the feud of years gone by color their impression of each other. He was excited to be part of the change here.

He trudged along the edge of the field, checking the fence as he strolled. It looked good. As soon as the house came into view, his excitement grew. By god, he owned a farm. And, he had a girl. Not just a girl, his dream girl. She was all the things. Smart. Kind. Beautiful. All the things.

He saw Spencer up on the ladder near the barn and sauntered over to see how far he'd gotten today.

"Hey there. How did it go today?"

Spencer came down the ladder and pointed to the camera. "I've got a camera installed on each corner of the barn. The wiring is all run. I had to wait until the horses were out today. I'm sorry, I spooked one of them this morning waving the antenna around. She thought I was going to whip her. I'm still mad at myself for that."

"Was Everleigh nearby?"

"Yeah. She and the veterinarian were here and got things under control quickly. It never occurred to me, Henry."

Henry chuckled and patted Spencer's shoulder. "Don't worry about it. If they managed to get things controlled, it's all good. These things will happen from time to time until the horses are used to us and know they're completely safe."

"Yeah." Spencer then stepped into the barn. "I also have cameras in each corner in here. There's a separate one in the tack room. And one in the feed room. Tomorrow, I should be able to hook everything up."

"Wow, you've been working hard."

Spencer shrugged. "We all are. Kenna's on her way out to see the place. I hope you don't mind that I invited her."

"Of course not. Besides, I don't think she's met Everleigh yet, so it'll be great for them to meet."

Henry glanced out the door. "Speaking of, where is Everleigh?"

"I don't know."

Henry shrugged. "I'll find her. It's nearly dinnertime. Mom texted me."

"Okay. As soon as Kenna gets here, we'll come in."

Henry sauntered to the house, he could hear the laughing and chatting wafting out here. He loved that. It had been like this his entire life. Everyone together. He hoped Everleigh liked having people around. It had been different for her.

He clomped up the steps. His feet felt like they weighed a hundred pounds. Inside the aroma of food made his stomach growl.

Yvette was the first person he saw. "Hey, Henry. How did you do this afternoon?"

"We did great. We've got two fields completely fenced."

"That's fantastic."

He shrugged. "How did you do this afternoon?"

Yvette laughed. "We got every dish in the kitchen pulled from the cupboards and washed. The cupboards have all been washed out and lined and the dishes put back in. I can't speak for the others, but I think Isi and I did a damned good job."

He chuckled. "It sounds like it."

Yvette finished putting something in the linen closet and went back to the kitchen. He followed her.

His mom looked up from something on the counter and scooted through the people and to him. "Hi. Did you have a good afternoon?"

"I did. I'm hungry and I can't find Everleigh."

His mom giggled. "She is taking a shower. Apparently Queenie decided to be a bit of a, well, a queen and gave her a bit of trouble. She came back to the house covered in horse doo and looking rather defeated."

He grinned. "That's gonna happen. I'll go see how she is."

He made his way up the gleaming staircase, still in disbelief this was his. He stepped into the bedroom to see

Everleigh sitting on a chair in the corner, putting on tennis shoes.

"Hi. I heard you had some trouble."

"Ah, well, trouble, I'm not sure. But, let's say, Queenie and I had a war of wills today."

He chuckled. "Who won?"

She tied her shoe and stood. "I think I did. But it was neck and neck for a while. She dragged me through a pile of horse shit out in the pasture. She refused to follow commands. She tried stomping me. She was as stubborn as stubborn could be. In the end, I jumped on her back, carefully, and rode her bareback to the barn. I think that surprised her, and in the end, she decided I wasn't so bad. Tomorrow, we'll do things differently."

He wrapped her in a hug and squeezed her close. "You feel good."

Her arms squeezed him back. "You do too. But you smell."

They both started laughing and he stepped back. "I'll go hit the shower."

"I think it's time to eat."

He kissed her lips. "I'm fast. Go on down. Spencer invited Kenna to eat with us. I'm happy you'll finally get to meet her."

"Me too. I'll see you down there."

They sat on the front porch after everyone had gone for the day. It was a nice way to end the day and he hoped they'd always enjoy it.

"Dr. Emily says the horses are all healthy and there's no reason they can't be bred. Tomorrow, I'll start searching for some sires. A couple of the horses have great lineage, so I'll find sires that have equal lineage. We should have quality foals to sell."

"That's wonderful. We don't need to hurry anything along though."

She turned to him with a gorgeous smile on her face. "I'm not in a hurry. It usually takes months to find an appropriate sire and then to get on said sire's schedule. So, it won't happen overnight. Plus, the gestation period for horses is eleven months or so. We won't see foals for a good year and a half."

"Wow. Okay. That will give us some time to get some beef cattle here too. What do you think of chickens?"

"I prefer them fried."

He burst out laughing. "Me, too."

She took a drink of her seltzer. "I think we can manage chickens. We'll need to do a bit of work on the coop though. It seems a bit run-down."

He glanced to his left where the chicken coop stood. The weeds had grown up around and inside it and he could actually see through it in one spot. He nodded. "Yeah, I'll have a couple of the Hickory Hills guys work on the coop tomorrow."

"How are they doing?"

"Fantastic. They're hard workers."

"That's great."

The sun sank into the fields, and he stood and held his hand out to Everleigh. "Let's get some sleep."

Her smile was a combination of good things to come and serenity. He loved that smile.

———

He woke to the horses making noise in the barn. He heard the neighing and kicking. It sounded as if something was distressing them. Everleigh sprang out of bed and tossed her clothes on before he could.

"Wait for me, Ev."

She flew down the stairs and out the door. He looked out the window and saw her run across the driveway and to the barn. He grabbed his boots and shot down the stairs. "Fuck."

His feet wouldn't move fast enough.

46

Her heart beat so fast she thought she'd pass out. It was that distressed sound she'd heard this morning when Spencer had the antenna in the barn. They were scared.

She opened the service door and stepped inside. She flipped the light switch on, but nothing happened. Up and down she clicked the switch, but the lights wouldn't go on. She pressed her hands to her back pockets, but she'd forgotten to grab her phone. "Shit."

She opened the tack room door and turned the switch on in there. Enough light glowed out to illuminate a portion of the barn. Enough for her to make her way to the horses. That's when she heard, "Don't take one more step toward these horses or I'll kill all of them."

"What?"

"You heard what I said."

Her brain scrambled. Who was this? His voice was familiar. "Case, is that you?"

She dared to take a step closer. Her eyes were beginning to adjust but the fear running through her body had the goosebumps on her arms raised higher than a kite. Her breathing came in spurts. "What do you want?"

"I want you to stop meddling in things that don't concern you."

Her brain snapped and cleared. "Craig?"

"I want you gone. You've created a mess that will take me years to clean up."

"The change is happening, Craig. You can't stop it."

"The fuck I can't." His face came into view. It was contorted, his mouth was a set line of determination she'd never seen before. "This is my mountain. Do you understand. Mine. It's my birthright. I waited years to be the president of Hickory Hills. My father was part of the resistance that formed the BRR. I'll not step aside and let some little bitch that never set foot here before to suddenly waltz in and take it all away from me."

"I haven't taken anything away from you. The people want change. Your people want peace."

"WE HAD PEACE." His voice was so loud the horses spooked and kicked the stalls.

She swallowed the hot rock that had formed in her throat but she conjured her true negotiating voice. "Can't you see they want something different?"

"It's not your concern. You don't even live here. You're just the whore that buck inside the house is using until he gets all he wants from you."

Her body shook as his ugly words spewed from his nasty mouth. "Gerard and Jasiah want peace."

"They don't fucking know what they want. Gerard is spineless. My wife's family wasn't raised to take over something as important as this. They are not my blood. Not my seed."

"But they are now in charge. In your absence they are in charge."

"What the fuck is wrong with your head woman? I'm not absent. I'm standing right here."

"But you aren't up there."

"I know where I am you fucking twat." His breathing came in short bursts.

Her stomach rolled. She was also just about finished with his name calling. She'd dealt with a scared stubborn horse and was successful. She'd deal with this asshole now. A sound came from the back of the barn and Craig whirled around. It was the first time she'd actually seen where he was standing.

Harper kicked at her stall again and Craig yelled. "SHUT THE FUCK UP YOU MISERABLE BAG OF GLUE."

Everleigh inched forward. She knew where he stood now. If the horses would calm down she could hear him too, but they were stressed.

Another noise sounded from the back of the barn and the back door slid open. "Who the fuck is back there?"

"Craig. This stops now."

"Gerard. You've got to be fucking kidding me. You're not going to stop me from doing anything."

"I believe I am."

Craig laughed. He sounded completely deranged. He wasn't thinking clearly. He was reacting instead of acting. She knew this from her years as a negotiator. He was more dangerous than most. He had nothing to lose.

She slid back to the tack room and searched around for a gun. Hopefully Henry had stashed a gun somewhere. She couldn't find one.

She pressed her back against the wall and inched her

way out of the barn. Gerard and Craig were still arguing, and she needed to find a way to get them out of her barn.

She kept her back to the stall doors as she moved toward Craig. The lights in the barn flickered then came on, low at first, but they grew brighter.

Craig whirled around and saw her standing near Harper's stall. He took two steps toward her but Gerard grabbed the back of his jacket and pulled him back. Craig fell on his ass but jumped back up and lunged at Gerard. The two men fought and the barn door opened once more. Henry entered and yelled. "KNOCK IT OFF."

Her heart raced and relief slid down her spine, though the goosebumps on her arms still stood tall.

The men froze and Craig pushed away from Gerard. She stared at Henry, but he was watching Craig. He filled the doorway, and she could hear in his voice that he was pissed.

"Ev. Come towards me."

She wanted to stay near Harper so she'd calm down. She hesitated and Henry's voice grew louder. "Ev. Now."

She swallowed and her breathing threatened to stop completely she was so scared. Craig pulled a gun and pointed it at her chest. "Stop right there, bitch."

She froze as she stared at Craig's gun. She'd never had a pistol pointed at her before. She'd never gone through anything like this before outside of her military training. And then, she knew she wouldn't be hurt.

Her knees wobbled and she didn't know if she could take a step if her life depended on it. Her stomach somersaulted and she worried she'd vomit. She knew she couldn't run fast enough to not get shot. The slight ringing in her ears filtered out many sounds.

The horses kicked at their stalls with force. Such force

she worried they'd injure themselves.

"Your girl isn't going to make it tonight, Henry."

Henry raised his gun and pointed it at Craig. Craig turned his head and laughed at Henry.

Gerard's voice called out to Craig. "We're finished with you Craig. You're the one who won't make it tonight."

Craig turned and laughed at Gerard. "You've got to be shittin' me. You? You aren't going to do a fucking thing Gerard."

"I'm making it right. All of it."

A shot rang out and she held her breath. As if in slow motion, Craig crumpled to the floor. His gun slid a foot or so away from him and she stared at the lifeless eyes of Craig Howard as they stared at her.

Harper burst from her stall and trampled over Craig's body before she could get her bearings. Harper ran out of the barn door and toward the pasture.

Everleigh finally gasped in a deep breath of air as she held on to the stall door behind her. It was then she noticed Gerard lower his arm and drop the gun in his hand.

She turned to see Henry, big burly, handsome, slowly stepping toward her. His eyes roved over her face. His jaw was tight, but he continued toward her. He'd holstered his gun and reached his arms out toward her.

She fell into his arms as the sobs wracked her body.

His arms circled her and he held her tightly. "Are you alright, Ev?"

She could only nod.

She felt the rumble in his chest as he spoke softly. "Are you alright, Gerard?"

"Yes."

"Sit down if you need to."

"I don't need to sit."

Henry held her close as her crying slowed. She pulled herself together and stood up straight. "I have to go find Harper."

"Wait for me. We'll go together after the sheriff leaves."

"How does he know to come?"

Her brows knit together.

His brows rose into his hair. Yeah. He'd called. He always knew the right thing to do. "And you need to stay here as you're a witness."

"Oh."

47

His heart stilled to the point he thought he'd die. Seeing Craig point a gun at Everleigh made his breathing stop. His brain felt like it had an electric current running through it as the worst possible scenarios zipped around his brain. It took him a few minutes to get his head on straight. This was his line of work, saving people. The hardest thing he did was set his personal feelings aside and move into work mode.

When Gerard shot Craig, the relief that flooded his body was undeniable. For so many reasons. For so many people.

Gerard stood stock-still as Henry comforted Everleigh. He pulled a bale of hay to the end of the barn so she didn't have to look at Craig's face. He pulled another one over for Gerard.

"Take a seat, Gerard. The adrenaline will wear off soon enough."

Gerard's eyes finally met his and Henry nodded. "It's going to be alright. Self-defense."

"He wasn't pointing the gun at me."

"It lends itself to the defense of others also."

Gerard's shoulders relaxed and he finally slumped down to the bale of hay.

He watched Gerard for a few minutes, then turned to Everleigh.

"Are you alright?"

Her eyes sought his. "I think so."

"It'll take a while for the adrenaline to leave. I'll get you a blanket. You'll likely get cold once that happens."

He stepped into the tack room and pulled a wool horse blanket from one of the hooks. He wrapped it around her shoulders and sat next to her. He wrapped his arms around her shoulders and waited quietly as the sheriff's sirens grew closer.

"Will he be okay?" He glanced at Everleigh and saw she was staring at Gerard.

"He will. There was really no other way this could go."

She nodded her head. They sat for a while. The crunching of the tires on the driveway reached his ears. Everleigh looked up at him. "Thank you for protecting me."

"It's my job, Ev."

A tear fell from her eyes. He swiped it away with his thumb. "I don't mean you're my job. I mean, it's my job to protect you. First it was a job. Now it's my duty. I will always protect you. For the rest of my life."

More tears fell.

The sheriff called from the outside. "Is it okay to come in?"

Henry kissed Everleigh's forehead, then stood. "Yes sir. Come in. Weapons are down."

The sheriff entered the barn. His eyes fell on Craig

Howard first. Then on Gerard at the end of the barn, then they floated to Everleigh.

"Henry. Why don't you talk to me first."

"Yes, sir."

"First, let me call an ambulance."

Everleigh asked. "Can you call Dr. Emily? Maybe she can search for Harper."

The sheriff huffed out a breath, pulled his phone from his pocket and called the department first. He asked dispatch to call Dr. Emily. Then he and Henry stepped to the side and had a conversation.

"What happened here?"

"Craig came looking for Everleigh. He's lost everything. He had nothing to lose. Gerard somehow knew he was here, I don't know how. You'll need to ask him that."

"Okay. So tell me what happened."

He retold his story, his eyes watching Everleigh and Gerard as he did. The sheriff didn't seem too bent out of shape about it all. He knew this was the likely outcome the way tensions were running too. Truth be told, there'd likely be few tears at Craig's funeral. He was an asshole, pure and simple. The bruises on his wife told that story well.

As the sheriff spoke to Everleigh, he called his dad. They likely heard about the shooting by now. But they knew better than to come guns running when the sheriff was here unless they were called.

"Are you alright? Is Everleigh?"

At the mention of Everleigh's name, his knees began shaking. He took a seat on a stool in the tack room. "My god Dad, seeing a gun pointed at her made me lose my training. I never want to feel that ever again."

"I'm aware."

He cleared his throat. "She's being interviewed now. I'm sure it'll take some time for her to settle tonight. And Harper burst from the barn. Dr. Emily is out looking for her."

"I can help with that. It'll help me burn off the adrenaline. I'll stop by later. Or, if I find Harper, sooner."

"Thanks, Dad. Tell Tate so he doesn't worry."

"He's in the living room right now with the others."

He swallowed the emotion that thrust up his throat. He had people who cared. A lot of them.

The instant the sheriff finished with Everleigh, he went to her and sat beside her. He placed his arm around her and she laid her head on his shoulder. He kissed the top of her head and held her close as he watched Gerard speak to the sheriff.

He had heard Craig bitching at the men who'd come down here to work today. He beat on a couple of them until they finally told him where Henry and Everleigh lived. Gerard followed him. Good thing too.

Another truck pulled into the driveway and an ambulance crew entered the barn. Photographs were taken of Craig's body. The procedures were followed, and he was loaded onto a gurney and whisked from the barn. There was a small amount of blood on the apron of the barn. It was amazing how so little blood actually ever seeped from a bullet wound. Television shows made it look like there were gallons. In truth, very little actually bled from the victim. A gunshot wound was made by a hot round of metal. It seared the entrance, and exit if there was one, and basically cauterized it. So, unless it nicked a major artery, there was little. In this case, not much more than a tablespoon.

Henry stepped over to it and sprinkled the blood with

lime. The lime would soak it up and, in the morning, he'd scrape it off with a shovel. They'd air out the barn to get rid of the sulfur residue that hung in the air. The horses had settled but he knew Everleigh wanted to calm them and would see that each one was okay before she went to sleep for the night.

With Craig's body gone, she began her rounds and he stayed by her side.

Footsteps approached with the telltale sound of a horse walking alongside. He and Everleigh turned to see his dad walking into the barn with Harper. He'd fashioned a rope around her neck and calmed her enough that she walked with him.

His dad nodded. "We just walked three miles. She was grazing down the road. Dr. Emily is on her way. She must have jumped the fence in her fright. You'll need to check the fence tomorrow before letting them out."

Everleigh approached Harper slowly. Harper's eyes were wary, but she allowed Everleigh to pet her nose and snuggle next to her neck. After a few minutes, Everleigh led her to her stall and she entered without a fuss.

Henry looked at the stall door. She'd broken the latch, so he used rope to tie it for the night. First thing tomorrow, he'd replace the latch.

"Thanks, Dad."

"Happy to help. Are you both alright?"

He glanced down at Everleigh and she nodded. "We're good."

He hugged his dad, tightly. Tighter than he ever had. His appreciation of what it meant to have people you could count on had increased a thousand-fold tonight.

Everleigh stepped forward and hugged his dad too.

"Thank you. For everything. I've never really had people I could count on."

"You do now."

She sniffed and he hugged her close once again. His dad turned to leave. "Wait, Dad. How did you get here?"

He pointed to Harper. "I walked. My truck is three miles down the road."

"I can give you a ride."

His dad grinned. "I called your mom. She was sitting with her phone in her hand. You know."

He chuckled. "Yeah. I know."

Tires on the driveway alerted them to her approach and he walked out of the barn with Everleigh tucked tightly to his body.

His mom stepped from the truck and ran to his dad first. They hugged. He kissed her lips lightly. Then she ran to him and Everleigh. She wrapped her arms around them both and hugged them together.

EPILOGUE

He watched Everleigh as she stood before him. "Should you push or pull? What's supposed to happen here?"

"I can't push and I don't think I should pull. It won't do any good. Where the hell is the doctor?"

He looked around helplessly. Harper moaned and Everleigh's brows furrowed. She petted Harper's neck. "It's okay girl. You're doing good."

When her eyes met his, he shrugged and mouthed, "Is she doing good?"

Everleigh shrugged. "I don't know. It seems like she's struggling."

Dr. Emily finally ran into the barn and came directly to the birthing stall. It had been set up as Dr. Emily requested. She listened with her stethoscope. Felt around Harper's belly. Then looked at her bottom.

She pulled on a long pair of gloves and squirted a gel on them. "Okay. I think the foal's hooves are blocking its exit. So, I'm going to reach up inside and see if I can straighten them out."

Everleigh's eyes rounded and landed on him.

"What do you need us to do?" He asked.

"Everleigh, you keep talking calmly to Harper. Henry, stand by in case I need some muscle."

He watched from outside the stall as Dr. Emily gently reached up inside Harper and maneuvered the foal's feet so they could come out. Harper moaned and Everleigh continued being a good midwife. Finally, Harper pushed and the foal's front two legs protruded from the birth canal.

"Good girl, Harper. Good girl."

Harper caught her breath and pushed once again. The foal's head protruded and Dr. Emily cleared its nose of mucus. "She'll likely only need one more push. I'll guide the foal out."

The doctor moved herself so she could help pull the foal from the birth canal as Harper caught her breath.

She lifted her head and began pushing. Dr. Emily gently pulled the foal free from the birth canal. Dr. Emily lifted its back leg and cheerfully announced. "You have a little boy."

He laughed and tears fell from his eyes. That was amazing. New life right here in their barn.

Everleigh patted Harper's neck. "You're a mommy. Congratulations, Harper. You have a little boy."

After a few minutes of resting, Harper struggled to stand up. Dr. Emily pulled her gloves off and reached down for Everleigh. "She'll want to clean her foal and check him over. You should step out now."

Everleigh stepped from the stall and threw herself into his waiting arms. "We have a boy!" Her eyes were wet with tears, too.

"I heard." He hugged her tightly as they stood and watched Harper lick her baby and nudge him to move.

Everleigh laughed. "Oh my god. I've seen horses born before. But this feels different."

He chuckled. "It does. He's ours."

He kissed her lips and they stood for the longest time just watching. Harper did all the things a good mother should do and Dr. Emily was happy with her progress. She packed up and left them alone with instructions on care. Harper would need special vitamins for a few days. But she'd feed her baby.

Once they were sure all was well, the other horses were fed and watered, he walked with Ev to the porch, where they dropped happily in their rocking chairs and stared out at the pasture.

"My emotions are all over the board right now." She whispered.

"Mine too. But before we end our day..." He knelt down in front of her. "Everleigh Hayes, will you marry me?"

He pulled the ring he'd been carrying with him for the past week from his pocket.

The serene smile on her face was his answer. But, just to be sure, she said. "Yes."

It was simple, but perfect.

His fingers shook as he slid the ring on her finger. Her lips shook when he kissed them. He pulled her up and twirled her around on their porch. Then he pulled his phone out, turned on the song he had ready to play, and Chris Stapleton's, "Tennessee Whiskey" began playing, as he held the love of his life in his arms and they danced on their front porch. Life just kept getting better and better.

ALSO BY PJ FIALA

You can find all of my books at https://pjfiala.com/books

Romantic Suspense

Rolling Thunder Series

Moving to Love, Book 1

Moving to Hope, Book 2

Moving to Forever, Book 3

Moving to Desire, Book 4

Moving to You, Book 5

Moving On, Book 6

Rolling Thunder Boxset 1, Books 1-3

Rolling Thunder Boxset 2, Books 4-6

Military Romantic Suspense

Second Chances Series

Designing Samantha's Love, Book 1

Securing Kiera's Love, Book 2

Bluegrass Security Series

Heart Thief, Book One

Finish Line, Book Two

Lethal Love, Book Three

Wrenched Fate, Book Four

Lynyrd Station Protectors - Security

Finding His Fire Book One

Finding His Mark Book Two

Finding His Jewel Book Three

Finding His Match Book Four

Big 3 Security Boxset, Books 1-3

Lynyrd Station Protectors - Special Ops

Defending Keirnan, LSP Special Ops Book One

Defending Sophie, LSP Special Ops Book Two

Defending Roxanne, LSP Special Ops Book Three

Defending Yvette, LSP Special Ops BookFour

Defending Bridget, LSP Special Ops Book Five

Defending Isabella, LSP Special Ops Book Six

LSP Special Ops Box Set One (Books 1-3)

LSP Special Ops Box Set Two (Books 4-6)

Lynyrd Station Protectors - Trafficking

RAPTOR Rising - Prequel

Saving Shelby, LSP Trafficking Book One

MEET PJ

Writing has been a desire my whole life. Once I found the courage to write, life changed for me in the most profound way. Bringing stories to readers that I'd enjoy reading and creating characters that are flawed, but lovable is such a joy.

When not writing, I'm with my family doing something fun. My husband, Gene, and I are bikers and enjoy riding to new locations, meeting new people and generally enjoying this fabulous country we live in.

I come from a family of veterans. My grandfather, father, brother, two sons, and one daughter-in-law are all veterans. Needless to say, I am proud to be an American and proud of the service my amazing family has given.

My online home is https://www.pjfiala.com.
You can connect with me on
Facebook: https://www.facebook.com/PJFialaAuthor
Instagram: https://www.Instagram.com/PJFiala.
YouTube: https://youtube.com/@PJFiala
TikTok: https://www.tiktok.com/@pjfiala?lang=en
If you prefer to email, go ahead, I'll respond - pjfiala@pjfiala.com.

COPYRIGHT

Printed in the United States of America

First published 2023

Fiala, PJ

PROTECTING EVERLEIGH / PJ Fiala

p. cm.

1. Romance—Fiction. 2. Romance—Suspense. 3. Romance - Military

I. Title – PROTECTING EVERLEIGH

ISBN-13: 978-1-959386-52-0

Printed in Great Britain
by Amazon

26003153R00183